KT-420-184

MERFOLK

To my brother Andrew, with love

Thank you for all the advice and videos
about diving in the Firth of Clyde!

Kelpies is an imprint of Floris Books
First published in 2021 by Floris Books
© 2021 Lindsay Littleson

Lindsay Littleson has asserted her right under the
Copyright, Designs and Patent Act 1988 to be
identified as the Author of this Work

 Also available as an eBook

British Library CIP data available
ISBN 978-178250-737-6
Printed and bound by MBM Print SCS Ltd Glasgow

 Floris Books supports sustainable forest management
by printing this book on materials made from wood that
comes from responsible sources and reclaimed material

MIX
Paper from
responsible sources
FSC
www.fsc.org   FSC® C117931

SECRETS OF THE LAST MERFOLK

LINDSAY LITTLESON

Kelpies

PROLOGUE

The rocky islet was silvered by moonlight and the sea glimmered, deceptively calm. All the others were asleep. Even Mol, their leader, was snoring, his sleeping face still stern.

As Muir drew closer her courage began to skitter away, a fish fleeing a shark.

Behind her, her brother Traigh whispered, his voice a hiss in the darkness, "Keep going."

Traigh had been reluctant at first to get involved in Muir's plan, but she had persuaded him, and so here they were, drawing ever closer to the highest rock, staring at a small, tide-carved cleft near the base, trying to summon the courage to steal from Mol.

This natural shelf held their leader's only possessions: a thousand-year-old shell box and an ancient flint arrowhead. Mol rarely looked at his treasures, and that fact comforted Muir a little. They should be able to return the box before he noticed its absence. As her fingers curled around it, Mol stirred and murmured in his sleep. She froze.

"Grab it. Quick." There was a hint of glee in Traigh's voice, as if stealing from Mol pleased him, however dire the consequences of being caught. And Muir could see why, she really could, because she felt the same. Every new moon a council meeting was held on the high rock, and every time she and Traigh were excluded. The elders said they were too young. Well, it was time for change. And while making that change was terrifying, it was also exciting.

As she clutched the shell box her fingers tingled, like a jellyfish sting without the pain.

"Got it."

Traigh stared at the box, his eyes round as moons, as if he couldn't quite believe she had gone through with it. He pointed across the expanse of dark water, to where lights twinkled on the far shore. "What if nobody answers our message? We will have risked everything for nothing."

Muir spoke as firmly as she could. "We have got to do something. You know that better than anyone. You have seen Her."

"You are right." Her brother gave a deep, sad sigh. "Let us go now. We need to be back before the others wake."

Silently, they slid off the rocks and into the sea. As they dived underwater, their long tails flicked.

1

FINN

When Dad swore, Finn stopped playing *Alien Wars* and glanced up from his phone. Snow was splattering against the car's windscreen. The wipers were flailing, struggling to keep the glass clear. Outside, the road was turning white. The sea cliffs had vanished, obscured by cloud and falling snow. Their route looked dangerous, but there was one upside to the worsening weather: at least Lizzy would stop wittering on about the views. Her constant commentary had been doing Finn's head in.

"Oh look, a sign for Culzean Castle! We'll need to visit! Look, it's Ailsa Craig, can you see it in the distance, Tom? That big lumpy rock! It's covered with bird poop because it's a sanctuary for seabirds like gannets and puffins."

Luckily Finn's dad had kept his eyes on the road, or they'd have gone over the edge by now.

Lizzy had tried to encourage both back-seat passengers to admire the scenery too, but Ava had been fast asleep by the time they reached Ayr, her head lolling against the car door, and Finn would have refused to cooperate even if Lizzy had pointed out something genuinely interesting, like an alien spaceship or a herd of sodding unicorns. There was no way he was playing Spot the Poo-splattered Rock.

Now Lizzy turned around, twisting her neck like a barn owl. She gave him one of her bright, fake smiles. "Nearly there! The satnav says Dunlyre is just over a mile away."

Finn dipped his head and stared at his phone but, as always, Lizzy failed to take the hint.

"Do you know this is my first trip to this area since I visited the Heads of Ayr Farm Park as a child, way, way back a zillion years ago?" She laughed, a high-pitched squawk as fake as her smile. "It rained the whole time and I was frozen to the bone!"

Finn pointed at the window. "The weather's looking bad right now. Maybe we should head home."

Lizzy laughed again and Finn felt his muscles tense.

Stop laughing. I'm not joking.

"Anyone would think you're not keen to spend Christmas with me and your dad!"

Finn gave her a look – a look he hoped told her everything she needed to know.

I love spending time with my dad. But you're the last person in the world I want around at Christmas, or New Year, or birthdays, or any other days, special or otherwise. I want you to get lost. You've wrecked everything.

Lizzy's smile slipped, but her voice stayed upbeat. "There's no point us going back home when we're nearly there, you silly cookie!"

She faced the front again but kept chattering. Finn grimaced. Lizzy never stopped talking. She was worse than his gran's budgie, who, Finn remembered, had been eaten by her neighbour's cat. Next time they visited Edinburgh Zoo, Lizzy might venture too close to the tiger enclosure… One shove and his problems would be over.

"We're going to have a fabulous time in a beautiful cosy cottage!" she trilled. "Imagine toasting marshmallows in front of a roaring log fire. It's going to be perfect."

Finn opened his mouth to remind her that he was twelve, not four, but caught his father's warning glance in the car mirror. He flushed, remembering the scene last month. Dad's voice had been firm, and his eyes sad. "Finn, I love you to bits. But I'm really disappointed in your behaviour. You need to stop being rude to Lizzy. It's upsetting her very much. She's so keen that you two get on. And she's my wife, Finn. I'll not have her insulted in her own home."

9

Finn had been about to answer back, ask if Dad meant he'd leave Lizzy behind on outings from now on, or if he meant that Finn could say what he liked about her when they were out of 'her own home'... but he'd thought better of saying anything at all. He'd even apologised to Lizzy, afraid she'd persuade Dad to leave him out of their weekend access visits.

But resentment was burning a hole in him. He couldn't share his feelings with anyone, not even Mum, who didn't seem as devastated by the break-up as he'd imagined she would be. In fact, she was infuriatingly upbeat.

Your dad and I haven't been getting on for ages. Splitting up was for the best. But just because we're getting divorced, it doesn't change the way we both feel about our kids. We love you both so much. Come on, Finn, sweetheart, don't look so sad. Look on the bright side, you'll have two bedrooms instead of one!

His mum didn't have a clue. Having two bedrooms was a total pain. The stuff he needed always seemed to be in the wrong place.

And there was no point moaning to his wee sister. While Ava had been distraught last summer when Dad left, she'd been easily bribed. She loved all the weekend trips to McDonald's, the zoo and the cinema. She adored her bedroom in Dad's flat, which Lizzy had made hideously girly, with fairy lights and a fluffy pink carpet.

And Ava, who doted on Disney films, thought Lizzy's unruly red hair 'looked like Princess Merida's'. In this war, Ava was a collaborator, not an ally. But it wasn't her fault. She'd been fooled by Lizzy and had no idea she was more Maleficent than Merida.

Finn was jolted from his thoughts when Lizzy shrieked, "We're here! There it is! Turn right!" Even satnav woman couldn't get a word in edgeways when Lizzy was around.

Dad veered to the right and the car slithered down a narrow road, the Wayfarer dinghy on its trailer swinging behind, past large houses, all with massive windows overlooking the Firth of Clyde. Though right now, nothing was visible through the fog. They'd planned to go sailing, him and his dad, but it wasn't looking likely in this weather. Then as Finn gazed at the filmy mist, it tore like thin gauze and for a moment he had a view.

Someone's in the water.

Finn drew nearer the glass. There was no way anybody would be daft enough to go swimming in weather like this. Maybe they were in trouble, he worried, rubbing at the window, trying to remove the condensation. But they didn't seem to be. Strong, bare arms were cutting through the waves. Someone, confident and competent as an Olympic-medal-winning swimmer, was striking out to sea. And they were swimming without a wetsuit, oblivious to the cold, the fog and the falling snow.

It's impossible. Nobody would be crazy enough to go out so far in water that cold.

He rubbed again at the window, but the fog had drifted across the sea. When Lizzy yelled again, Finn jumped so hard he nearly dropped his phone. "This is it! The big stone one!"

Dad swerved into the drive, and as soon as he pulled on the handbrake, Lizzy undid her seatbelt and leapt out.

"We've arrived!" she yelled, banging the roof so loudly that Ava stirred in her sleep.

Finn dropped his phone into his rucksack and tugged at the zipper. "You don't say," he muttered.

Dad whipped round, annoyance creasing his forehead. "Behave yourself. None of your lip this week, do you hear me? Ava, wake up, sweetheart! We're at our holiday cottage."

Finn pulled a face. If Dad was dumb enough to wake Ava mid-nap, he could deal with the whining. He'd clearly forgotten Mum's mantra: 'let sleeping Ava lie'.

He stepped out of the car, dragging his rucksack behind him, and shivered in the intense cold. A biting sea wind nipped at his nose, and as he looked up at the house, flecks of snow spat in his face.

It wasn't his idea of a cottage. He'd imagined something like the Three Bears' house: small, quaint and thatched, with roses around the door, although maybe not in winter. This place looked brand new: blonde sandstone, pale wood and enormous windows. His trainers sank into the snow and he felt cold wetness seeping into his socks. The expensive boots his dad had bought for him would be useful after all, and he was relieved he hadn't left them behind.

Lizzy was fiddling with a key, and as he reached the porch, the front door swung open. She beamed at him, weirdly determined to keep up a friendly facade in the face of seething hatred.

"Cross your fingers that the gorgeous photos on the rental website weren't faked!"

Finn stalked past her, flashing a false smile in case Dad was watching from the car, and found himself in a large, warm, open space. There was a big living area with a massive coffee table and two huge leather sofas at one end, and a kitchen with a range cooker and a long dining table at the other. The front and back walls were almost entirely made of glass, the sea view at the front obscured by falling snow. An oak staircase led upstairs. Finn hoped the upper floor had proper rooms so he could have his own space, or he'd insist on sleeping in the car.

He was about to check when Lizzy tugged at his arm. He stiffened and she jerked her hand away, as if she'd been electrocuted.

"Sorry. I just got so excited about the tree. Isn't it beautiful?"

He could hardly miss the massive Christmas tree standing by the fireplace, festooned with fairy lights and sparkling glass baubles, but he wasn't about to agree with Lizzy. The tree was great, he could admit that, to himself at least. If Mum was here, and Lizzy a stranger living on the other side of the planet, he'd have felt excited about skipping two days of school and spending time with his parents in this stunning, festive house by the sea. But Mum was in Lanzarote with her 'friend' John, and that was a whole different level of worry.

He rubbed his forehead, as if that would make his problems vanish, and glanced round the room.

"There's no telly." A terrible thought occurred to him. "Has this place got Wi-Fi? Because if it doesn't, we can't stay."

Lizzy laughed. "Of course, it's got Wi-Fi. Tom's worse than you. He can't stand to be out of touch. And of course, he'll need to be in regular communication this week. This harbour development means a lot to him."

Finn dropped his rucksack on to a fluffy sheepskin rug so large it must have been made from an entire flock.

"What harbour development?"

He wasn't speaking to Lizzy. His words were directed at his father, who'd come in, hair wet, nose red, carrying Ava over his shoulder. Finn's sister was wailing, drumming her fists on Dad's back, though not nearly as hard as he deserved.

"Dad, what development? Are you working this week? Is this not a holiday at all?"

His father's expression told him everything. He'd been lied to, again.

2

SAGE

It was snowing inside the living room. Actually *snowing*. Tiny flecks were sneaking through the gaps in the log-cabin walls, spinning across the room and dissolving in the warmth. Taj danced around barefoot, his curls bouncing as he tried to catch the snowflakes on his tongue, while Sage pulled the shawl tighter over her shoulders. The cabin their parents had rented for the winter was small, and she didn't love sharing a bedroom with her wee brother, but up till now it had seemed solid enough, and it was cosy when the living room fire was lit. Now it was clear it wasn't even weatherproof.

"Normal people don't live like this."

"Normal's boring!" Taj yelled. "Wait till it hails. Hailstones will be zipping through the walls like bullets!" He demonstrated ducking and diving, dodging imaginary bullets, knocking Sage's book off the table.

She narrowed her eyes at him. "Watch it, Taj! You need to calm down. You've got actual cabin fever."

Taj cocked his head, baffled, and then shouted for their mum. "Zara! Come and see! It's snowing!"

Zara popped her head round her bedroom door. She'd been in there for ages, knitting needles clicking. "Yes, it's getting bad out there. I hope Kate's okay. She's been gone for over an hour."

"No, it's not just snowing outside." Sage waved a hand at the dancing flakes. "In here. We've got actual snow in the actual house."

Zara's eyes widened, and for a moment Sage thought snow in the house might be the last straw, but no such luck. Instead, their mother was having a brainwave. Scooping up one of her multicoloured rag rugs from the floor, Zara fetched a hammer and nails and tacked the rug across the wall. It didn't even wrinkle when a gust of wind rattled the windows.

"Problem solved, and it looks great too. Really colourful. Should have thought of it before. We could sell them to the shop as wall hangings." She gave Sage a triumphant grin and ruffled Taj's curls. "Taj, go and fetch your reading book."

Taj pouted and kicked at the table leg. "It's nearly Christmas. We don't have homework this week."

"Why on earth not? School isn't over for another two days. Go and get a story from the bookshelf then and read that. Sage, my lovely, will you go and shut the hens in their coop? I let them out for some fresh air earlier, but I'm worried about that fox. She was prowling round last night, I'm sure of it."

Sage sighed but didn't argue. She was fond of those daft hens, and come spring, hopefully they'd lay eggs. Then she remembered that by spring her family would have moved on, and the hens would be sold, or eaten.

Still, she couldn't let the poor souls be a fox's dinner, so she unwrapped herself from her cocoon of quilts and blankets, shivering, and grabbed her wellies. As she pulled on her jacket, Zara handed her a lime-green woolly hat.

"Brand new. Fresh off the knitting needles."

Sage pointed at a neat stack of hats on the shelf. "Don't you want to put it in the shop pile? Hats will be flying out the craft shop in this weather, and with Christmas so close."

Zara laughed. "We can call it an early present. Merry Christmas, my lovely girl."

When she wrapped her arms around Sage and squeezed, Sage breathed in her warm scent: cinnamon, because Zara had been baking cookies, and lavender oil, because she dabbed it on her wrists to help her sleep. Soft hair brushed Sage's cheek and gave her a sudden twinge of anxiety. *I'm the same height as Zara! Next year I'll be starting high school, and I won't know anyone. I can't even remember how many primary schools I've been at. How many times will I be the new girl in high school?*

Taj slapped his book down on the table. "Why didn't I get an early present? It's not fair. I want a laser sword."

Sage met Zara's eyes and her mother winked. "When you've done your reading, lovely boy, you can have an oatmeal cookie."

Satisfied, Taj opened his book and began to stumble over the words. Sage bit her lip. Poor Taj had no chance of a laser sword. It would be home-made gifts or nothing for Christmas. And even if they hadn't been skint, a toy weapon was out the question. Their parents always said, "We can't make a peaceful world if we encourage children to play violent games."

Sage tugged at the front door and jumped when somebody behind it spoke: "Excellent timing!"

Red-nosed as Santa's reindeer, her other mother, Kate, was standing on the steps, a proud grin stretching from one rosy cheek to the other. Kate's blonde curls, glistening with snow, stuck out under another of Zara's knitted hats.

"I've made it through the blizzard! I feel as proud as Scott of the Antarctic, reaching the North Pole!"

Sage laughed and held the door open to let Kate through. "Don't think so. Captain Scott was raging cos he didn't get there first, and it was the South Pole, not the North. And anyway, you've only been to the newsagents."

"Nobody likes a smarty-pants." Kate stuck her tongue out and waggled her hands.

"Very mature, Mother."

"Close the door, you eejits!" yelled Zara. "Did you get the paper, Kate? Any news on the you-know-what?"

"It's Sunday, you numpty. Nothing ever happens on a Sunday. It'll all kick off tomorrow."

Sage rolled her eyes, pushed the ill-fitting door closed and walked down the two rickety steps. She looked back at the cabin and sighed.

I really don't care about the 'you-know-what'. Enough's enough. We need a proper home.

Let's face it, Cliff Lodges was a dump, not much better than the caravan in which they'd lived last spring. Zara said the rent was next to nothing, but no wonder. The owner planned to renovate the cabins once they'd left, and her exact words had been: "I need to bring them up to scratch if I'm going to rent them to tourists." At the moment the cabins were little more than hovels, and incoming tourists meant Sage and her family would have to be out by March, whatever happened. Her mums hoped the harbour development would be stopped once and for all this week. Their plan was to move to Cornwall next. Neither of her parents had consulted Sage about the move. Or Taj, come to that, but it wasn't worth consulting Taj on anything other than dinosaurs or Lego.

Sage had heard only good things about Cornwall, with its rugged coast and surf-battered beaches, and the sea would be a bit warmer than in Scotland. But how would she get out there without her beloved kayak? She'd have to leave it behind because, strictly speaking, it didn't belong to her. The thought of living without it was unbearable.

And she'd miss Dunlyre too: the solid, dependable presence of lumpish Ailsa Craig, the quiet magic of the little harbour, the rolling hills and grassy cliffs. She'd even miss their shabby little cabin. In the last few months, it had become home.

It was tiring to keep moving about like this. It wasn't good for Taj, who didn't have any close friends his own age and who found it hard to settle in new schools. And to be honest, it was exactly the same for her. Being the new kids at school was horrible. They never seemed to have the right uniform, and often uniform was the least of their worries.

Sage trudged across the snow towards Zara's hand-crafted hen house, the one building that didn't need brought up to scratch. Snowflakes danced in front of her eyes, soft and light as swansdown, melting on her cheeks.

Inside the fence, the snow lay thick and pristine. There was no sign of their six rescued Gingernut Rangers. Sage's heart began jumping in her chest. What if she was too late? What if they'd rescued those hens from a hellish life in a cage on a battery farm just for a fox to murder them all? What if inside the coop was the scene of a bloody massacre, all blood and guts and ripped-off heads?

Her wellies made her clumsy, but she vaulted the low fence round the coop, hurried over to the door and flung it open. All six hens were perched, cosy and warm, snuggled up together, their feathers fluffed, eyes closed. Sighing with relief, Sage closed the door and fastened the little hatch, determined to keep her girls safe.

She started back towards the cabin, stepping in her own boot prints, but then stopped dead, and listened. The five cabins stood in a semi-circle bordered by trees, and they were all occupied by people who'd travelled here to protest about plans for the Dunlyre Harbour development. But nobody was outside, not on a day like this. There were no tourists about either, and all the locals were at home in their smart, weather-proof houses. Even the herring gulls had gone quiet. The only sounds were the low whoosh of the waves breaking on the rocks, and the noise that had made Sage stop: a strange, high-pitched singing.

The hairs on the back of her neck rose as she turned around and looked out towards the horizon. On the shore, far below, the sea sucked at the rocks. In the distance, on the cliff's edge, ruined Dunlyre Castle was a black silhouette against a pale sky. The singing seemed to be coming from that direction. Her throat tightened as she stood statue-still and listened. She'd heard the same sound for a brief moment yesterday, and had wondered if it was the wind blowing a hoolie as it surged in with the waves. But here it was again, even louder.

What the heck is that? A fox, maybe, or a feral cat?

But she dismissed the thought. The sound was too tuneful to be coming from an animal. Almost human, but not quite.

As Sage listened, she felt a tingling sensation in her limbs. Feelings of loneliness and longing swamped her brain, and tears stung her eyes. Then her tummy began to churn and her muscles tensed, like they did during the first day in a new school. Sage hugged herself tight, and then the painful feelings swirled into a glorious, bubbling excitement, and she closed her eyes and lifted her head skywards. Something new and life-changing might happen, if only she had the courage to—

Sage screamed like a banshee as something hit the back of her neck.

"Ha! Got you!" Taj jumped up and down with excitement and threw another snowball. She ducked sideways and the snowball thudded against her arm. Scooping up snow, she compressed it in her bare hands, the cold making her fingers burn, and sent her own missiles flying. The first smacked against his shoulder; the second hit him right in the face.

23

"Ooft… are you okay?"

For a second, Taj stood stiff as a snowman, face frozen in shock, and she wondered if he was going to burst into tears. But then he started to laugh and gather more snow. The battle was on!

It was only much later that evening, when she stood shivering in one of the shower block's narrow cubicles, trying to wash her hair under a pathetic dribble of lukewarm water, that Sage remembered the strange singing from the sea. Taj's screams and her laughter during the snowball fight had drowned out all background noise. And there had been so much chatter during dinner that the sound had been pushed to the back of her mind.

As she tugged on her clothes over still-damp skin, she could hear the song, reverberating in her memory, but wasn't able to rekindle the wonderful glow of anticipation that had swirled over her. There was something oddly familiar about the song, she realised. She closed her eyes, trying to remember. Zara had sung something similar when she told one of her favourite folktales, the one about the merfolk from the land of Cianalas. It was a favourite tale of Zara's – she'd grown up near Dunlyre and had happy memories of listening to her dad telling the story round campfires on the beach. When Zara had sung, Sage had been able to conjure images of the merfolk, the waves lapping their great fishtails as they sang their sad songs on the rocks.

Did I hear them singing today? Could there really be merfolk here in Dunlyre?

She had to towel-dry her hair, because the hairdryer wasn't working again, and as she stood at the mirror, her reflection gazed back at her, confusion etching frown lines on her forehead.

Maybe she was suffering from an overactive imagination. It wouldn't be surprising. Zara was always telling them stories, mostly with their roots in her grandparents' homeland in Pakistan, but also from other wonderful, faraway places around the world. Folktales about mythical creatures like the Chakora, a magical bird from Hindu mythology who lived on moonbeams and brought good luck, and the Chinese Qilin, a gentle, hooved mythical creature who cared for the natural world. And the merfolk, who'd been forced to adapt to life in the ocean after a tidal wave flooded Cianalas. When Taj had asked Zara how the merfolk breathed underwater, she had claimed the merfolk could hold their breath for as long as dolphins and spent most of their lives under the sea, but they sometimes liked to sit on rocks and sing sad songs, remembering their drowned world.

Zara also told them the merfolk cared for all the

creatures in the sea and on the shore, and got terribly upset about marine litter. Sage pulled a face in the mirror.

Can't help noticing Zara's stories always have a 'caring for the environment' theme. Funny, that. Me and Taj are being brainwashed by bedtime story.

When Sage stepped out of the shower block, the icy air fogging her breath and the security light dusting the snow with glitter, she stood still, listening. Martha, in the cabin next door, finished playing 'Silent Night' on her fiddle and began another carol. In the village, a dog was barking at the moon.

No singing, and no merfolk, because this is the real world, not one of Zara's myths. In the real world, birds don't live on moonbeams, and merfolk don't exist.

But as Sage trudged the few metres back to the cabin, memories of the song still echoed in her head. She had definitely heard *something*.

Someone or something was singing. But who?

3

FINN

When his dad didn't reply, Finn glanced at Lizzy and caught her mouthing the word 'Sorry'. Dad had been keeping secrets from him and now she'd let the cat out the bag. Anger burned in his chest and his fists clenched so hard his nails dug into his palms.

"Dad? What development? What's she talking about?"

"*She* has a name, Finn!" Dad's voice was tight.

One of his gran's daft sayings drifted into Finn's brain. *She's the cat's mother.* His gran had always had a saying at the ready. Her favourite was, *What's fur ye wull no' go by ye,* and every time she said it Dad would roll his eyes, and say, *That's a pile of mince, Mum.* And then she'd chase him round the kitchen, brandishing a brolly, or her handbag, shouting, *Get back here, ye big tumshie, ye're no' tae auld tae skelp*, while Finn laughed until his sides ached.

27

The memory stung, and he bit his lip, appalled by the tears nipping his eyelids. He missed his gran. After she'd died, his whole life had started to unravel. If Gran had still been alive, she'd have told Dad he was behaving like an eejit, sent Lizzy packing and talked Mum into coming home. Everything would still be okay. They'd still be a proper family.

Dad lifted Ava off his shoulder and tried to hug her, but she flailed around and wailed like a baby.

"Finn, we'll discuss it later, okay? I need to go and get the cases, before it gets dark. Ava, will you stop that screeching! You're nearly six, not two!"

His father placed Ava down on one of the massive couches, where she huddled against a cushion, body juddering with sobs. Her freckled face was streaked with tears and her eyes were red-rimmed.

"Where's Mum? I want my mummy!"

Finn sat down and put an arm round her shoulders. "It's okay, Avie. You were asleep in the car and now we're at the holiday house, with Dad. Nice, isn't it? Look at that ginormous tree!"

The tension in Ava's body eased. Her face brightened, as he'd known it would. She could be cheeky, but she wasn't a whiny, moody kid, like that wee monster his pal Dev was stuck with. Finn hated going around to Dev's flat because poor Dev had to share his bedroom with his brat of a brother and never got any peace.

Muumm! Dev and Finn are hogging the Xbox again! I want on! It's my turn! It's not fair! They've got biscuits! I want some!

Nobody would be able to hold Dev responsible for his actions if he lost his temper and chucked the wee ned out the window. Next to Dev's brother, Ava was a nice kid. The only time she was more of a menace than a swimming pool of piranha was when she woke up after a nap. Dad should know that, after spending all those years in the same house. Clearly, he hadn't been paying attention.

Ava gazed in awe at the Christmas tree, which was about three times bigger than the scraggy, tinsel-draped effort they had at home in Glasgow. She turned to Finn and grinned, showing the gaps in her teeth. "Where are all my presents? Why are they not under the tree?"

"It's too early, you wee numpty."

Lizzy, who'd been nosing around in the kitchen area, banging cupboard doors, called over. "They've left a few provisions for us. Who'd like a hot chocolate?"

Ava leapt up. "Me! Me! Me!"

Finn bit his lip. He'd kill for a hot chocolate, but…

"Sounds brilliant. We'll all have one." His dad staggered back into the house, carrying Lizzy's massive case, and his and Finn's much smaller ones. "Finn, can you get Ava's stuff out the car? Then we can have a chat about what's happening this week. The work side's not a big deal, I promise. We'll have plenty time for fun!"

"Yeah, right."

When Finn opened the front door, the cold smacked him in the face. The wind was howling now, and the snow was thick on the ground. Pulling up his hood, he ran towards the car, edged past the trailer so he could open the boot, and pulled out Ava's purple trolley case. With a reluctant shudder, he grabbed Mee-mee, his sister's filthy, smelly comfort blanket.

There's no way she'll sleep in a strange bed without it.

The word 'strange' made Finn think of the swimmer he'd seen earlier. He turned his head, glancing out to sea. Below the cliffs, the sea was a churning grey froth. The light was starting to fade. And, to Finn's astonishment, the swimmer was *still in the water*! He shivered in the cold wind, unable to comprehend what his eyes told him.

It's not possible. No one could survive out there for so long.

Possible or not, there was someone in the water, heading back towards the shore, undeterred by the crashing waves, and they seemed perfectly at home. The distance was too great for Finn to make out any details, but he was hugely impressed by their technique. Finn had been in the swim team since he was seven and considered himself pretty good – no, he was *really* good – but this swimmer's butterfly stroke was incredible. Muscled arms and shoulders propelled their upper body through the churning waves in smooth, undulating movements, while their legs were underwater, presumably doing the synchronised kick that was so difficult to master.

Finn was still staring when, without warning, the swimmer surged vertically out of the water, almost to mid-thigh level, then dived in a swooping arc. Head and shoulders plunged below the waves, the back followed and the entire body disappeared below the surface.

What the heck?

Finn had been leaning over the boot, watching the swimmer, but the shock of that incredible, dolphin-like dive jerked him upright so fast that he hit his head on the underside of the boot lid. Dazed and groaning, he loosened his grip on Ava's things. The trolley case thudded to the snowy ground and the blanket flopped after it. He grabbed at the trailer for support.

Swearing, borrowing some of the colourful words Dad had used earlier when somebody cut him up on the motorway, Finn tried to walk back to the house, but his dizziness was overwhelming.

"Dad!" he called, but the word was tugged skywards by the wind. He opened his mouth to try again, but a gust threw a clump of snow from the roof and made him stumble.

His father appeared in front of him and grabbed his arm. "Finn, what are you doing, lad? Why have you chucked Ava's stuff in the snow?"

"I… I banged my head. On the stupid boot lid."

His dad picked up the case, shook snow from the blanket and stuffed both under one arm. He used the other to hold onto Finn's elbow.

"Come inside. We'll get you an ice pack."

As Finn lurched back to the house, he felt like he might face-plant in the snow. When he opened the door and stood, swaying, letting freezing air swirl into the room, Lizzy gasped and grabbed his arm. She guided him towards the couch, talking to his dad as if he wasn't there, and he felt too wobbly to shake her off.

"What's happened? He's white as a sheet. I knew there was something up when he didn't come back right away. I thought he'd…" She didn't finish her sentence.

Does she think I'd run away? Leave my wee sister?

He sat down and his dad ran his fingers over his scalp. It hurt, quite a lot. Ava had grabbed Mee-mee and was holding the blanket up to her face, sniffing at the label, as she did when she was anxious.

"Is he okay?" Lizzy's face was creased with worry. It must be hard work, trying to pretend to Dad all the time that she cared about his kids. Finn knew she was lying. He'd heard her on the phone, the day she'd moved in with Dad.

"He's given himself a bump, and there's a bit of blood, but he'll not need stitches, which is just as well, eh?"

His dad pointed out the window at the darkening sky, the twirling snowflakes. "Wouldn't fancy my chances of getting the car out again in this snow, and heaven knows where the nearest doctor is."

Lizzy made a tsking sound with her tongue. "You shouldn't have sent him out in that weather, Tom! You should have gone yourself." She held up a plastic folder. "There's a surgery in Alloway, which is less than six miles away, and a big hospital in Ayr. All the information about the area is in this folder. There are some ice cubes in the freezer, Tom. Wrap them in this cloth. Ava, come and sit at the table to drink your hot chocolate, sweetie. Let your brother rest. Put your feet up on the couch, Finn."

Finn felt too dizzy to argue. Ava slid off the couch, still clutching her blanket, then draped the damp fleece over his legs. "There, there. You've got Mee-mee now, so you'll be all comfy."

His dad brought the ice pack over. Finn took it, but when he pressed the cloth against his scalp, the cold reminded him of being outside, and the swimmer he thought he'd seen. It wasn't possible...

He opened his eyes, just as his dad returned with a mug of steaming hot chocolate, and tried to explain. "Someone was in the water... I saw... I think they..."

"Here, drink this, son." His dad's voice was kind but tinged with impatience. *He thinks I'm a total eejit who can't*

33

do a simple job. "And then lie down and have a wee sleep."

Lizzy tsked again. "Oh Tom, he shouldn't do anything of the kind! It's important to check the responses of a child who's had a head injury, and we can't do that if he's asleep. Finn, do you still feel dizzy? How many fingers am I holding up?"

Finn resisted the urge to make a rude gesture with his own fingers, to tell her to mind her own business. "No, I'm okay. Three."

"Don't fuss over him, Lizzy. We'll worry if he starts seeing things."

Finn's hands tightened round his mug.

Was I seeing things that weren't there? Did I imagine the swimmer after I banged my head?

He had no idea. Perhaps it was better to say nothing, or Lizzy might insist they get back in the car and head for the doctor's surgery in Alloway.

The dizziness was easing, and the hot chocolate was warming his insides. He was feeling more like himself again.

Once Lizzy had been convinced that he wasn't concussed, Dad insisted Finn have an early night. There were proper bedrooms upstairs as he'd hoped, three of them, and his room was the best, because it had a huge skylight and a comfy double bed directly underneath. It even had a tiny shower room. He read for a while, and listened to music, and tried to stuff everything else to the back of his mind. Around ten o'clock, his dad came in to check on him.

"You feeling any better, son?"

"Yeah, I'm fine."

His dad plonked himself down at the end of the bed. "I know this… situation… has been difficult for you, Finn. If you want to talk, I…"

Finn groaned, and turned so his face was squashed into the pillow. It was hard to breathe. "Not now, Dad. I just want to sleep."

His father tiptoed out and shut the door behind him.

Finn turned onto his back, and gazed through the skylight. It had stopped snowing and shredded clouds were drifting across the moon.

Dad never told me what his plans are for this week. He's still keeping secrets from me.

His heart started thudding in his chest. Because something else was dawning on him. When he'd been out there, getting Ava's things from the boot, he'd been watching the swimmer for a couple of minutes, admiring his technique. He'd banged his head when he'd straightened up, startled by the sight of that amazing dive. He'd seen the swimmer *before* he'd hit his head, not after. He hadn't been 'seeing things'.

The swimmer was real.

4

SAGE

When Sage woke the next morning, the air in the tiny bedroom she shared with Taj was so frigid that she couldn't imagine ever being able to get out of her nest of quilts. And maybe she wouldn't have to… She leaned over the top bunk.

"Taj, go and look out the window. If it's still snowy, school might be off!"

Taj leapt out of bed and pulled aside the patchwork quilt they used as a curtain. "Snowmageddon! No school! We can stay in bed all day!"

The bedroom door creaked open and Kate shattered both their dreams. "Up you get, you two. Monday morning's here!"

"Nooooo!" Taj's voice was so high-pitched it reminded Sage of the strange singing she'd heard yesterday. In the cold light of day, it seemed ridiculous that she'd first thought of Zara's story.

Merfolk? In my dreams…

Taj was jabbing his finger at the glass, desperate to prove his point. "But Kate, look, it's a Snow Day!"

"No, it isn't. The radio says all roads are open and so are all of the schools in South Ayrshire. Come on, kids. It's only two more days until school stops for Christmas. You can do this!"

Sage empathised with every single one of Taj's groans of despair.

The living room was cosy, the fire blasting out heat. All through breakfast Taj kept whinging, but Sage ate her wholemeal toast, sipped her peppermint tea and didn't bother saying a word. There was no point trying to persuade her parents. Education was Everything: on the subject of school, Zara and Kate were like two separate humans with a single, shared brain. She and Taj had virtually one hundred per cent attendance, although they'd never stayed at one school long enough to get any praise for it.

"Bye, my lovelies." Zara handed over two beeswax cloth bundles containing their cheese sandwiches. Taj pulled a face. He stuffed the package into his bag, below his gym shoes and homework diary. Sage ruffled his hair, sympathising. It wasn't that her brother didn't like cheese sandwiches, but he wanted them in a Spider-Man plastic lunchbox like the other boys. He didn't want to be different, even when different was better.

When Sage and Taj opened the front door, they stepped into Narnia. Snow lay on the ground, clean and fluffy as a newborn baby's blanket, hiding the grass and the gravel paths. All the hard edges were blurred. Even the castle's jagged walls and the spiky gorse bushes on the cliff edge were downy with snow. In the distance, the sea gleamed, pink and glossy as mother-of-pearl in the dawn light.

It was bitterly cold.

Taj tugged at his sister's arm. "We could hide on the beach till it's time to come home. Pretend we've been at school."

"Don't be daft, Taj. We'd freeze."

Taj's lip jutted. "I saw people swimming in the sea last week, way out deep. They were in for ages, and they were *bare.*"

"No way. It's not even ten degrees in there. That's really cold. Unless they were wearing wetsuits, they wouldn't stay in the water for long."

"I did see them." Her brother gave her a conspiratorial look. "I think they were merfolk."

Sage felt her skin tingle and she struggled to keep her voice casual. "Did they have fishtails then, these swimmers?"

"Um, I don't know…" Taj sighed, realising his story had a serious flaw. "I only saw their arms."

"Merfolk aren't real, Taj." Sage laughed, relieved.

Taj kicked at the snow. It sprayed in an arc, splattering over her boots. He gave her an accusing look. "You don't believe in anything any more."

"Rubbish. What about Santa? The Loch Ness Monster? I believe in those."

"Well, duh. Course Santa's real. And the Loch Ness Monster is a giant eel, the one in Zara's story. That's what the scientists say. And merfolk are real too. Zara says so."

"Yeah, you're right, she does. But we're not going to the beach. We're going to school, so you'd better get a move on, kiddo."

By the time Sage and Taj got home from school, it was half past three and the sun was low in the sky. Dark would come quickly at this time of year, but Sage was desperate to look around for anything that might explain the strange singing, and she had a little time. While she was at it, she could check her kayak was safe after yesterday's stormy weather. And she was keen to have some time on her own. It had been a difficult day. School two days before the holidays was slow and pointless, and then at lunch a grumpy-faced boy at the school gates had called her a loser. He wasn't even a pupil, just some passer-by on the street. She'd stood up for herself and told him to bog off, but it had been upsetting, all the same.

Outside the cabin, Kate was attaching a length of rope

to a sledge made from an old pallet. "Zara and I are taking this girl out on her maiden voyage!" she called. "We're hoping to avoid icebergs. Who wants to come aboard?"

"Me, me!" Taj raced into the cabin to change out of his school uniform.

Sage shook her head at Kate. "I'll give the sledging a miss. I'm going to put the hens away and then go for a walk. I won't be long."

As soon as the hens were safe, she left Cliff Lodges and walked towards the castle, her boots crunching on snow. The path ran uphill close to the edge of the cliff.

Slowing her pace, Sage looked down and saw that the water far below was flecked with gold from the sinking sun. The tide was heading in, small waves swirling between rocks, the sea edging ever closer up the beach. At high tide the water reached the bottom of the cliff and the beach disappeared, becoming part of the underwater world.

All day, Taj's comment about merfolk had been floating through her mind. She'd figured he must have spotted a group of wild swimmers.

But now, she'd begun to have doubts.

It doesn't make sense. If they were wild swimmers having a dip, they'd stay shallow. If they were swimming deep, they'd be properly equipped. Nobody in their right mind would go swimming way out in winter without a wetsuit.

40

Maybe tomorrow she could head out in the kayak and see whether there was anything strange out there. Memories tugged at her of paddling through sun-splashed waves, the only sound the crying of the gulls. Out there in the firth you could spot sad-eyed seals bobbing their glossy heads out of the waves, or watch gannets divebomb, straight as arrows fired into the sea. Once, she'd even caught a fleeting glimpse of a dolphin flashing by, his mouth curved in an underwater smile.

Could Taj have seen dolphins? Hmm. Whales sing, don't they? Maybe dolphins do too.

She shielded her eyes against the low sun and stared out to sea, but today the waves seemed empty of life.

She sighed.

Face facts. Taj's head's full of nonsense. He probably made up the whole story.

Sage approached the ruined castle, perched like a giant crow right on the edge of the cliff. As she stepped into its shadow, a chilly feeling of impending danger crept over her like fog. From here, the cliff face looked steep, the winding path leading down to the beach dangerous, slippery with snow. She began to have second thoughts.

Maybe I should just head home. I can check the kayak tomorrow.

A movement above her caught her eye and she glanced up at the derelict tower. It was only a raven, flapping its

41

oil-black wings as it came in to roost, but it was enough to make her lose her footing, and she slipped, and went over the edge.

Frantic, her arms flailing, clutching at air, she tumbled down the slope towards the rocky beach. Her hands were clumsy in her woollen gloves, and even when she managed to grab a tuft of grass sticking out through the snow, it didn't stop her descent, only slowed it. Her body kept sliding, her only thought, *The rocks... the rocks... the rocks...*

The hillside fell away and, feet first, she dropped the last metre.

Pain shot through her jarred ankles and she yelped and half-fell, half-slumped onto a lichen-stained boulder. Leaning forward, overcome with dizziness and nausea and shock, she closed her eyes.

After a few moments she regained control of her breathing and opened her eyes, wanting to check her feet. Shoving her gloves in her pockets, she took the left boot off as gently as she could, shook out the snow and examined her ankle. No marks, no swelling, no sticking-out bones. The other foot looked okay too. It really hurt, but she felt that if she just waited, the pain would ebb and she would be able to walk over the rocks. Sage took a deep breath, head swimming with relief, and as her lungs filled with cold sea air, she felt herself come back to life.

You total numpty. So much for not going sledging.

Waves crashed against the rocks, getting ever nearer, but her ankles didn't feel up to clambering over the massive boulders on the shore yet. So, staying on her limpet-crusted rock, she turned to face the cliff. She spotted the almost-invisible cleft at its base at once. Yesterday's pounding waves hadn't reached it, and the narrow gap was still covered by thick tufts of snow-speckled seagrass. Her precious kayak was safe in its hiding place.

Excellent, my kayak's okay. Now I need to solve The Mystery of the Weird Singing.

Calmer now, Sage turned her gaze to the beach. But there was no mysterious singing, just the breaking of the waves and the cries of distant gulls. An icy wind was nipping at her cheeks.

The pain had eased to a dull throb, so she staggered to her feet and almost stood on a large shell.

Sage picked the shell up and held it in the palm of her hand. She turned it over, her brain whirring.

What on earth is this?

Though it had come from the sea, not the earth, so perhaps she was asking the wrong question. It was a large cockle shell, about the width of her palm: curved, ribbed and shaped like an old-fashioned fan. Whole – both halves still joined. But it was no ordinary shell. A tiny silver lock nestled where the two halves clamped together, and when she shook it gently, something rustled. The object was a box, and there was something inside.

5

FINN

Finn hadn't bothered to draw the skylight blind, and he woke, blinking, to sun shining in his eyes. When he closed his eyes again to protect them from the glare, he could see that incredible swimmer powering through the water, then leaping high and diving underneath the waves.

I saw it... I'm sure I did. That guy had skills. Maybe I'll be that good one day. Hope I get to do some wild swimming while we're here.

Barefoot, Finn padded across to his case and pulled out clean clothes. His stomach growled and he hoped there were bacon rolls for breakfast. Dad did an excellent bacon roll. But thinking of his father reminded him that his dad had been keeping secrets... telling lies. This holiday wasn't a holiday at all. If it was all work time for his dad, there was no chance they'd be going sailing or swimming together.

45

Slamming the bedroom door, Finn stomped downstairs.

Ava, still in her unicorn pyjamas, was at the big table, chattering away to Lizzy. Dad was on the couch, slurping coffee and reading the paper.

"Look Lizzy! I was right!" When Ava shouted, she spat cereal across the table. "In the mornings, Finn's as grumpy as the Gruffalo!"

He flung himself into the seat next to his sister and growled like a bear. "Don't eat with your mouth full, Avie. It's minging. If I was the real Gruffalo, I'd be having you for breakfast. Scrambled Ava on toast. Yum!" He put an arm round her shoulder and pretended to bite her nose. When she squealed like a train's brakes, his dad grimaced and rustled his newspaper.

"Good morning, Finn!" Lizzy's voice was irritatingly cheery. "Ava's having Frosties. Would you like some? Or Tom has made pancakes, if you'd prefer."

The bacon-roll dream sizzled and died. But pancakes were also good, and he managed four, drizzled with maple syrup. Then he put the plate in the dishwasher and went to tackle Dad.

Under interrogation, his father was forced to confess. He didn't give in immediately, of course.

"We are here on holiday, Finn. This is a Christmas treat for you and Ava. And me and Lizzy, of course." He swept his arm like a conductor's. "Look at this place!

It's gorgeous. When I was a kid, living in a council flat in Drumchapel, I could only have dreamed of staying somewhere like this."

Finn rolled his eyes. Gran had stayed on in the council flat in Drumchapel until the day she died. She'd loved her cosy home and would have been scathing about this house.

Everyone can see in the windaes! It's like living in a ruddy fish tank!

Dad must have spotted Finn's eyeroll. "Anyway, we've all worked really hard this year and deserve a little luxury."

Finn looked over at Ava and raised an eyebrow. She'd tilted her head right back so she could slurp the milk from her Frosties straight out of the bowl. This was not a person who had been working herself to the bone all year. Who was his dad trying to fool?

"Lizzy said you're here for work. Something about a harbour development?"

"Well, yes." Dad's gaze shifted to the left. "I'm hoping to squeeze in a tiny bit of work-related stuff this week. A couple of short site visits, just to see what's what, and a meet-up with the planning chaps in Ayr. A couple of hours, no more. No big deal."

Finn gave him a look, telling him he'd heard it before, and his dad bristled.

"Work pays the bills, you know. You'll understand better when you grow up a bit."

Finn tried to stifle his annoyance at his dad's condescending tone.

Maybe the work thing isn't a big deal. A couple of hours doesn't sound too bad. If it's true…

Dad gulped down his coffee and changed the subject. "Anyway, what are our plans for today?" He waved a hand towards the big expanse of glass. Through it, they could see the sea, glittering like crystal in the sunlight, and a bright blue sky. It looked almost tropical, apart from the snow in the front garden. "Perfect sledging weather, don't you think?"

Finn felt the weight in his chest lighten. It *was* perfect weather for sledging, and the rolling hills behind the house looked ideal.

But first Ava wanted to make snow angels in the garden, and then had to change into dry clothes. After that, Lizzy and his dad wanted to walk into the village. Dunlyre was pretty, with its quaint little harbour, cliffs and castle. They had lunch in the cafe at the harbour, and Lizzy insisted on visiting a craft shop and buying a daft woolly hat. Finn walked on ahead and swaggered past the village school, feeling quite superior to all the kids milling around, trapped behind bars like animals in a zoo. He stopped there, looking behind for Ava.

A girl in a too-big purple coat was standing alone by the playground fence, her long, dark hair whipped into tangles

48

by the wind, her hands in her pockets. When Finn spoke, she jumped, as if she'd been shaken awake.

"Who are you, Nelly No-Mates?"

He'd been attempting a joke, but she didn't smile.

"Bog off, why don't you?"

He bristled at her snappy tone. "It's a free country. I can stand here if I like."

But Dad and Lizzy were heading uphill towards him, with Ava skipping beside them, clutching the ice cream she'd insisted Dad buy her, because "It's a holiday," and Finn didn't want to be caught arguing with a stranger, so he started to walk away.

Behind him, the girl's voice rang out. "You should be in school!"

"I'm not a loser like you," he shot back, and strode off.

So Finn and Dad didn't drag the three sledges from the attached garage until about half two, but then they sledged for over an hour, shrieking and whooping down the hillside. Ava went on Dad's sledge the first few times but then insisted on going with Finn, "Cos he's fastest."

The fun lasted until she tipped off when he veered to avoid a rock. Finn sped past her, unable to stop, as his sister tumbled down the rest of the hill, screeching with terror.

Dad rushed over, his face ashen, and scooped her up. Finn jumped off his sledge, his heart hammering in his chest.

"Is she okay?"

"Jeez, Finn. What were you—"

"Ava's fine." Lizzy's voice was firm. "She's just had a fright and needs a warm bath and hot chocolate."

Is that her answer to everything? How does she know Ava's not hurt? It'll be all my fault.

"I wasn't asking you. I was asking Dad."

"That's enough!" Dad spun round, Ava still in his arms. "That backchat stops now! Do you hear me? You're going to spoil everybody's holiday if you keep this up."

Tears sprang to Finn's eyes. "It isn't really a holiday at all, is it?" He brushed the tears away on the back of his sleeve, mortified. "It's work, and you've dragged Ava and me along, so you don't have to feel guilty about leaving us at New Year while you swan off on a cruise with *her*. And I know she hates me and Ava, because I heard her say so on the phone! 'The two of them are a complete nightmare.' Remember?"

Lizzy gasped, a long intake of breath, and Finn felt heat flare on his face, knowing he'd gone too far.

Before Dad could freak, Finn hared off, running as fast as the snow and his heavy boots would allow. Behind him, his father was yelling his name, but he ignored him and clumped onwards, putting more and more distance between himself and the others. Their sledging hill was near the school, but the playground had emptied now, the pupils gone home. He wished he'd been at school today after all, and that everything was normal. He'd be home by now, watching telly, eating a pre-dinner snack, getting nagged by Mum to change out of his uniform. Lanzarote was nearly two thousand miles away. He'd checked it on Google.

Why couldn't she just have gone to Blackpool?

As he skidded down the steep hill towards the harbour, pain gripped his insides like a vice and tears nipped his eyes, salty as seawater.

The weather had changed again. Clouds had massed, dark and mountainous, and a sharp wind was biting, sending the harbour's weathervane into a spin.

The harbour was deserted, except for an old couple sitting at one of the picnic tables by the wall, their collie lying beside them. They'd cleared the snow off the table, but even so they were a bizarre sight, with their coffee thermos and sandwiches, wind whipping at their scarves, and reddening their noses. The dog leapt up and started barking as Finn ran past.

"You're in a hurry, son!" laughed the old man. Finn didn't respond, although he did slow down. The sea was right in front of him, waves smashing against the harbour wall. He leant over the wall, gasping for breath, trying to figure out why he hurt so much. It wasn't a stitch, it cut deeper than that. It felt like homesickness.

He breathed in damp, salty air, tried to clear his head.

Yes, he wanted to go home, but he wanted home to be the place it was before. Now, Mum was constantly plumping cushions because "John's coming over and the place is a tip," or putting on lipstick because "I'm having a well-deserved child-free night." Maybe the thing that hurt most was the feeling that, nowadays, he was always in the way.

Spray from a crashing wave dashed against Finn's face, as if someone had chucked a bucket of cold water at him. A memory came into focus: standing with Gran at the window of her flat, grinning and waving at Ava, who'd just arrived with Mum in the car.

Och, look at the way the wean's eyes light up when she sees you, Finn! The rest of us might think you're a pain in the bahookie, but that wee yin thinks you're God's gift.

The pain in Finn's stomach eased a little. No matter what the adults said or did, Ava would always want him around.

Wiping tears and spray and snot from his face with his jacket sleeve, Finn stared out to sea. The strength of the wind made it hard to breathe.

There's something out there.

He leaned further, trying to get a better view.

More than one something. Is it… could it be… a pod of dolphins?

Spray slapped against his face, soaking his hair, and the wind dragged him backwards, but he held on and kept staring, wishing he'd brought the binoculars he'd spotted hanging on a peg in the porch.

It was getting harder to see, especially in the dimming light. Finn straightened up and rubbed at his eyes, nipped by the salt spray, and noticed something he had missed before: a battered pay-to-view telescope attached to the harbour wall, just a few metres away. Rummaging in his pocket, he found a pound coin and pushed it in the slot. He swivelled the telescope, and he saw them. Far out at sea, two figures were cutting through the water.

Not dolphins… People.

Finn could see the flash of bare, muscled arms. They were wild swimmers, butterflying through the frothing waves. It looked as if they were racing each other. A swimming competition in freezing water. His dad wouldn't approve at all. He thought that ice milers were crazy, risking their lives for a dare, as Finn had discovered when he'd suggested they do an ice mile together.

"There are hardly any rules, Dad! We just need to swim a mile in water that's five degrees Celsius or less, wearing normal swimwear and goggles. Come on, Dad. We can do it."

"Don't be silly, Finn. You know what can happen to people in freezing water, don't you?"

Finn had persisted, because he'd been really keen. "It's just a mile, Dad!"

"Yeah, but it's often the first few seconds that kill." His father had run a hand through his thinning hair, frowning. "The shock of the cold makes people fight for breath and that's when they swallow water. They die of drowning before hypothermia gets them. You should know all about this stuff, son. I've told you often enough."

Finn had realised he was wasting his time, but tried anyway. "I know. But we could train, couldn't we?"

"Maybe, but what's the sense in it? Serious training over several winters is essential, and why take the risk? For a buzz of adrenalin? No way. We'll carry on being sensible and keep our wetsuits on. Deal?"

Looking through the harbour telescope, Finn realised his dad might have been right. Though he was an excellent swimmer, he was nowhere near as amazing as these crazy ice milers. Their bodies arced through the waves, movements perfectly synchronised. Finn watched, unblinking, and then gasped.

One of the swimmers plunged underwater, his entire body disappearing below the choppy waves. The other swimmer followed, sending an arc of spray shooting upwards with one flick of a long, dolphin-grey tail.

For a long moment Finn stood, clutching the telescope, staring out to sea, feet frozen to the ground. Behind him he could hear the elderly couple calling to their dog and walking back to their car. The old people had been totally oblivious to the incredible sight he'd just witnessed. He should have called them to come and look, but it had been over in seconds. And now Finn was left struggling to believe what he'd seen.

Merpeople don't exist. They're only in stories. I'm seeing things.

He put a hand to his head to feel the tender spot where he'd whacked it against the car boot. He rubbed it gently, suddenly afraid.

I've got concussion. Dad should have taken me to the doctors last night, but he couldn't be bothered. I'm seeing stuff that's not there, and it's all Dad's fault.

Cold, but determined not to return to the holiday house, Finn made his way behind some cottages, and started back uphill. He could see the castle in the distance.

After he crossed a narrow bridge, the way got steeper, slippery with snow. He was nearly at the dark ruin when he stopped, realising he was being watched. A girl in a too-big purple coat was standing perfectly still just a few metres away, her long, dark hair whipped into tangles by the wind, her hands in her pockets. She was looking straight at him, and there was a frown on her face.

Oh, heck… this isn't even a wee bit awkward.

It was the girl from the school playground, the one who'd told him to bog off… The one he'd called a loser.

6

SAGE

The climb back up the hill from the beach seemed impossibly slippery, so Sage walked along the increasingly narrow shore to the harbour, taking it slowly, trying to avoid the largest rocks. It was hard going with her sore ankles, and when she reached the harbour, she hesitated. It was almost deserted, except for a boy leaning so far over the wall he looked as though he might fall in the water, and an elderly couple who ambled past her on the way to their car.

The old woman smiled at Sage. "Daylight's fading. Time to head home!"

She knew it was time to go and feed the hens, and her ankles ached, but she wanted one last look at the sea from above. She wanted to solve the mystery of the singing. So she limped back along the clifftop to the castle, keeping to the path, taking care not to stray too close to the edge this time, her ears still tuned to hear the strange singing, remembering last night's magical feeling of anticipation and excitement.

A sound behind her made her turn, and that's when she saw the boy from the harbour heading across the little stone bridge, stomping like a troll. She watched him as he trudged uphill and wondered what he was doing out here by himself in the almost dark. And then it dawned on her...

It's the same boy... the rude one who was outside the school.

He'd almost reached the top before he noticed her. His shoulders were hunched, his face scrunched in a scowl, like Taj when he didn't get his own way, or when his Jenga tower collapsed.

The boy spoke first. "You again. Are you spying on me or something?"

What the heck is his problem? He doesn't even know me.

Sage laughed in his tight, set face. "Eh, no, I live here. You need to chill. Go roll around in the snow. That should do it."

He bristled, spiky as his hedgehog hair. His scowl remained firmly in place. "You were watching me. I saw you." The boy's eyes were narrowed, his expression sour. Resentment seethed from him like steam from a geyser.

She'd have told Taj, "Hold that expression while I fetch a camera," but she had a feeling that wouldn't go down well, so she frowned back, fixing the boy with her hardest Paddington stare. "Well, we're quits then. You were gawping at me earlier when I was minding my own business in the playground."

She was about to stick out her tongue and leave, head in the air, but something made her pause. She'd watched the boy from the playground fence as he'd re-joined his family. She'd seen him take his wee sister's hand and make her laugh, fake-crying that he didn't have an ice cream too.

There was a nicer lad hidden behind that scowl.

"You shouldn't have called me a loser."

The boy winced and a scarlet flush seeped across his face, so Sage kept talking. "But I shouldn't have told you to bog off. Like I said, we're quits."

Giving him her sunniest smile, she pointed at the ruined castle. "I come up here sometimes to get peace and quiet from my kid brother. Is that why you're here? To get away from your wee sister? I saw your family earlier. Your dad was clutching a map. It was hard to miss your sister's neon-pink jacket and your mum's hat, which my mum knitted, by the way." She paused. "So, what *are* you doing up here?"

He didn't reply. He'd gone very still. The singing had started up again, and it dawned on Sage that the boy could hear it too. Relief flooded her chest, warm as bathwater.

I'm not going crazy. Someone is *singing.*

Sage moved a little closer. "You can hear it too?"

58

For a long moment he didn't answer, and she wondered if she'd got it wrong. The lady walking her Labrador only a few metres away seemed totally oblivious, and maybe the boy was too. Maybe the mournful, high-pitched song was only in her head.

But when she looked at him, she saw his expression had altered and his hunched, defensive body language had vanished. His head was tilted to one side.

"I know it'll sound daft." The boy's face reddened. "But I can feel these sounds, as if they're travelling through my feet and rising upwards through my body. It's very weird."

Sage nodded. It didn't sound daft to her at all. During reiki, healing energies coursed around the body. Maybe sound energy could do the same? When Zara told her stories about the merfolk, she said their songs had healing powers...

And Sage could definitely feel the song's energy flowing through her own body, drawing out emotions. A deep sadness that something was lost and couldn't be replaced, mixed with a niggling fear of the unknown. But as before, these feelings quickly vanished and were replaced by a spine-tingling anticipation. Was the boy feeling the same things? How could she ask, when it was almost impossible to explain?

She tried, knowing her words were inadequate. "It's a bit like the feeling I used to get on Christmas Eve when I was little."

The boy nodded, and his eyes met hers. "Yes, like something amazing's about to happen! But it's more than that, isn't it? Not as straightforward, somehow. It's like, amazing things will only happen if—"

He stopped, as though, like her, he was unable to find the right words.

"If we're brave enough." She finished, and then laughed, feeling silly. "So, not like Christmas at all. But you're right, it's very weird."

The singing seemed to have got even louder, more insistent. It was amazing that the entire population of the village wasn't rushing to see what was going on. But when Sage looked at the houses beyond the football field and the car park, front doors were shut and Christmas tree lights glowed in windows. Nobody else seemed aware.

"Where's it coming from, do you think?" He spoke in a whisper.

"I don't know." She shrugged her shoulders, then listed the explanations she'd considered… except one: "I heard it last night too. I thought at first it might be foxes. Or dolphins or whales in the firth. What do you think?"

"Dolphins make clicking sounds." He paused. "I thought I was hearing things, but I guess if you can hear it too…"

Her fingers brushed against the shell box in her pocket. *Will he think I'm mad?* She took a deep breath. "My mum would say it's the merfolk."

There was a long silence.

Great. I should have kept my mouth shut. Now he thinks I'm crazy.

When the boy finally spoke, he sounded puzzled. "What the heck's a 'merfoke'?"

Sage felt her cheeks flush. "Merfolk. It's plural. One merman or mermaid, several merfolk."

For a moment his eyes widened, and Sage thought he believed her, but then he curled his lip, and her heart sank.

"Ah, right. Fish-people… I saw those in a movie. They're made-up. Not real."

Sage turned away and shook her head. "The merfolk aren't fish." She stopped and glanced at the boy, worried she was sounding completely mad. But his sneer had vanished. He was staring out to sea, as if searching for something.

"What, so they're mammals, like humans and dolphins. They breathe air?"

"Yeah, I guess so. Dolphins can stay underwater for about twenty minutes, so maybe it's the same for the merfolk. Who knows?"

"And you think these merfolk are real? You've seen them?"

Despite the cold, she could feel heat creeping up her face, conscious she'd made a fool of herself. "N-no, of course not. I mean, they're not really real. It's a folktale.

The merfolk are mythical creatures, like unicorns and dragons."

He turned and looked at her, and she caught a flicker of uncertainty in his eyes. "Yeah, obviously."

Sage's fingers tightened around the shell box.

It isn't, though. It isn't obvious at all. Someone is singing down there. I have this weird object in my pocket. Something very strange is going on.

The boy's eyes met hers. "At the harbour, earlier, I thought I saw—" He fell silent and stood, listening. With his head cocked to the side, and in his bright red jacket, he looked like a robin on a Christmas card, but less cheerful, and much less cute. "The singing's stopped."

She nodded. "Yes, it's stopped. And I need to go. I'm meant to be checking on the hens."

"Yeah, I'd better head home too, and say sorry to my stepmother. Again."

So he'd had an argument at home and run off. That explained the bad mood, at least.

"Bye. Enjoy your holiday."

Sage started to walk away. Her ankles ached, and she wasn't looking forward to the walk home, but felt reluctant to end things here. Despite his prickly exterior, there was something oddly likeable about this boy. If there *were* merfolk out there, she wanted to find them, and she'd like his help. She knew nothing about him, but in a strange way they were connected: apparently the only two people in the world who could hear the singing.

She turned back to the boy. "What's your name, by the way? I'm Sage Malik."

"Sage? Really? Like the herb? Wow." His face was transformed by his toothpaste-advert grin and the sparkle in his eyes.

"Yeah, like the herb. Sage is supposed to be great for bloating and flatulence, so that's nice."

He laughed. Actually laughed aloud, and the sound made him seem like someone she could be friends with, not someone she'd cross the street to avoid.

"Parents, eh? My name's Finn. I was named after a footballer who played for the team my dad supports. Star striker, apparently, until just after I was born, when he was dumped from the team for drug taking."

"Nice."

"Look, Sage, why don't we meet up tomorrow, down on that beach below the cliff? We can't just leave it like this. We need to find out what's going on, don't we? Check we're not actually going crazy."

"Sure." Sage felt warm inside, and smiled, despite her efforts to stay cool. "Though it's always possible we *are* both going crazy."

"True fact." He grinned at her. "See you tomorrow. Two o'clock?"

"Yeah. See you, Finn."

All the way home, Sage clutched the shell box in her hand, like a good luck charm.

7

SAGE

When Sage limped through the cabin door, Zara was pulling her boots on. "I was just coming to look for you!"

Sage closed the door, shutting out the cold air. The thought of going out again later to have a shower wasn't appealing. "No need. I'm back."

Kate smiled and waved a dishcloth. "Dinner's in the oven. You should have come sledging. It was brilliant. Did you enjoy your walk?"

"Yeah, it was good. I'm starving." As she tugged off her boots, she winced, and Zara noticed right away.

"What's wrong? Have you hurt your foot?"

"No, don't fuss. I'm fine, honest."

This was such a fib that she felt herself reddening, and had to turn away towards Taj, who was sprawled on the couch, holding action figures engaged in a loud battle to the death.

"Taj, when Spider-Man has finished murdering Iron Man, do you want to make Mrs G something for Christmas?"

She knew the other kids would be coming in tomorrow morning bearing beautifully wrapped little gifts – candles and chocolates and Best Teacher mugs – and didn't want Taj to be empty-handed. She knew what that felt like.

He grinned. "What about a witch's hat? Or some anti-wart cream?"

"Don't be mean. You need to stop that, Taj. Name-calling's mean. It hurts people's feelings."

He looked up at her, and there was an odd, closed look in his eyes she'd never seen before, and didn't like at all. *Has somebody been calling him names? Are the kids at school bullying him?*

She took his arm and pulled him off the battered couch. "Come and sit at the table and we'll make her a nice card."

Half an hour later, the card was completed and the table was smeared with a sticky film.

"Can you clear up that mess?" called Kate. "We're going to have dinner. But keep the art materials handy and we can create some more mess tomorrow. We need placards for Wednesday afternoon's protest. I've been reliably informed that Duncan McPherson is planning to visit the harbour with a news camera crew, so we'll need to be there, making ourselves heard."

Taj's eyes gleamed. "I'll smack the bad man in the face with mine!"

Sage put a hand on her brother's shoulder. "When did you turn into a wee ned? Go and wash your manky hands at the sink. It's pasta bake. Your fave!"

After dinner, Sage slipped into her bedroom for a moment to take a closer look at the shell box. In the lamplight the lock gleamed, smooth and shiny against the shell's rough ridges. Carefully, she slipped the end of a pen lid into the tiny gap between the shell halves and tried to prise them open. But they were clamped together, held tight by that tiny lock. Defeated for now, Sage slid the shell under her pillow.

I'll take it with me when I go back to the beach tomorrow.

She helped Kate wash the dishes while Zara sat by the fire, knitting yet another hat. When they'd finished, Sage went over and sat on the rug by her mother's feet.

"I know you've told it a zillion times, but could you tell us the folktale about the merfolk? I feel like a fish tale tonight."

Taj cackled at her terrible joke, clambered onto Zara's lap and burrowed his face in the folds of her shawl.

"Yeah, tell us about Kee-An-Al-Us."

"Cianalas is a Scottish Gaelic word that means

homesickness, or longing," Zara began.

That feeling swept over Sage, a peculiar mix of loneliness and homesickness, even though she was in the living room of her own home. She was too big to climb onto her mothers' laps, too old for long, comforting cuddles. She was growing up, and she didn't feel ready.

Then Zara's voice broke over her head like a wave.

"The story of the merfolk of Cianalas begins in the Land Time, when human beings lived in caves and hunted woolly mammoths, and merfolk didn't exist."

Sage sat by the fire, listening intently, yearning to believe, as her mother's soft, melodic voice flowed.

"The people of Cianalas were hunter–gatherers, living among the mammoths and the sabre-toothed tigers and the aurochs, until one terrible day, disaster struck. A gigantic wave crashed over Cianalas and flooded the land. All the people and the animals that had once lived happily on land were taken by the sea."

Taj lifted his head from Zara's shawl and grinned evilly. "Sploosh! Bye bye, Cianalas! Bye bye, mammoths!"

Sage rolled her eyes. "Taj. Don't be horrible." She looked at Zara, whose eyes were sad.

Wonder if she's thinking about the poor souls caught in an ancient tsunami, or worrying about Taj?

"It must have been horrendous." Sage shivered, imagining it happening to her own family, the terror they'd feel as the massive wave rolled towards their cabin, tearing up the trees, crushing their home to matchsticks. She imagined being dragged away from them by the force of the wave and swept, screaming, out to sea. "Those poor people."

Zara nodded, and even Taj looked chastened.

"Yes, tragically, many people and animals lost their lives." Zara was silent for a moment, and then continued her story. "However, and here's where the merfolk's history begins, some of the people didn't drown when the land was flooded. Instead, they transformed."

Sage pulled a face. "Aw, come on. They would have drowned before that happened, surely?"

Zara smiled, firelight twinkling in her dark eyes. "I expect there was magic involved, don't you think? The fact is, that it happened, one way or another. Their legs became tails and they could spend a long time underwater."

Taj caught Sage's eye. "Told you so." His voice was a stage whisper. "Told you merfolk exist."

She shrugged. "Maybe. Maybe not."

He stuck out his tongue at her, mischief dancing in his eyes, and she did the same back. It dawned on her that her wee brother would be thrilled if she told him about the mysterious object she'd hidden under her pillow. He'd be convinced it was merfolk treasure and would be so excited. But he'd be completely unable to keep the 'treasure' a secret. And once her parents realised that she'd been on the beach alone in the half-dark, they'd stop her from going again. And if they learned about the kayak she'd found, they'd be furious. Imagining her mums' dawning horror made her shiver.

You've been using it? In the sea? On your own? Without telling us where you were? Sage, that's unbelievably dangerous! You could have drowned. How long have you been lying to us?

And they'd be dead right… That was the terrible part. It was reckless and dangerous to go kayaking alone. But… she was good at it, and being out in the kayak made her happy. She couldn't give it up and so she wouldn't tell Taj about the shell box. Some secrets had to be kept.

Zara gave Sage's hair a gentle tug. "If you two listen quietly, I'll tell you the rest."

"The scary part." Sage leaned against her mother and watched the flames flicker, as Zara continued the story.

"Sabre-toothed tigers were no longer a threat, but in their new underwater world, the merfolk faced an even more terrifying enemy: Easgann Mòr, an enormous, eel-like sea monster. Even before the drowning of their lands, the people of Cianalas had been petrified of Easgann Mòr, and when they sat round their fires they had told stories of her wicked deeds: how she would rear up out of the water, blood-red jaws wide, and swallow swimmers whole, how she would capsize boats and drag the drowning sailors to their deaths. Their bravest had tried to defeat her, but she was longer than a minke whale, her snake-like body the girth of a tree trunk. Now, the merfolk were in constant danger from this ferocious sea beast."

"And sharks?" asked Taj. "Weren't the merfolk scared of sharks?"

"No, merfolk aren't scared of sharks. It is only Easgann Mòr they fear. She is the only creature that can harm them, because her power is more ancient than the merfolk's, who are otherwise immortal, which means each one lives forever, they never grow old.

The Great Eel had taken the Drowned Lands as her territory. When she finished scavenging on dead animals, she turned on the merfolk. Many were killed and eaten. Terrified, all who survived were forced to leave the Drowned Lands and the bones and relics of their dead."

Zara's voice sounded mournful, as if she was describing a terrible memory of her own.

"One night, while Easgann Mòr was asleep in her lair, the merfolk fled north, where they found a small island off the Scottish mainland, and hid there for thousands of years. Easgann Mòr followed but, unable to find the merfolk, had kept swimming north, where she settled off the Icelandic coast, capsizing longboats and feasting on Viking sailors, who knew and feared her as Jörmungandr, the Midgard Serpent.

A thousand years ago Easgann Mòr, badly scarred by

her encounters with brave Viking warriors, swam back to Scotland, and this time she discovered the merfolk's hiding place. Another massacre took place, too terrible to describe."

The wind rattled the windowpane, and Sage shuffled a little closer to the fire. There was a long pause before Zara continued.

"Helped by a pod of orca, who shielded them from the eel's sight, the few surviving merfolk made their escape. They swam round the northern tip of Scotland to the west coast, where they live to this day, on the tiny islets among the selkies and the seals, the last of their kind. And, according to the legend, Easgann Mòr is still in the north of Scotland, hiding in the great lochs, capturing unwary fisherman and feasting on foolish children who enter the water alone."

Taj pulled a face at Sage, clearly feeling vindicated. "See, I told you so. The Loch Ness Monster *is* Easgann Mòr."

"Perhaps she is." Zara smiled, and ruffled his hair. "But whether she will stay there forever is anyone's guess. The poor merfolk must live in constant dread."

"Do the merfolk eat nothing but raw fish?" Taj screwed up his face. "Sushi looks minging."

"They eat raw fish, yes, but their main diet is shellfish. They pick the limpets off the rocks. They sing their sad songs. They remember all the tragedies they've experienced in the past.

"And they live in terror that one day Easgann Mòr will find them."

Sage glanced up, her heart beating fast, and asked a question she'd never asked before.

"Why do we never see the merfolk, or hear them singing?"

Zara didn't pause. "They have magic on their side, and can hide from people with ease. Legend says they asked a human for help once, long ago, and it ended badly. When the merfolk lived in the seas of the far north, over a thousand years ago, they approached a local fisherman and pleaded with him to capture Easgann Mòr in his nets, but the man was too afraid and refused to help. Since then, the merfolk have given up on humans. Instead, they care for the creatures of the sea."

Sage's heart was pounding, and her throat had gone dry. "How did the merfolk contact the fisherman in the north? Did they sing?"

"Yes, the fisherman heard the merfolk singing every night for a week and when he finally went down to the sea, they were waiting for him on the rocks and gave him a beautiful cockle shell. The fisherman made a silver lock for the shell, and the merfolk chief heralded the shell box as a symbol of friendship between the merfolk and humans. But when faced with the monster, the fisherman was too much of a coward to help, and he threw the shell box back in the water. He left the merfolk to their terrible fate."

As Sage sat, every nerve tingling, Taj asked the question he always asked when Zara talked about merfolk, as if hoping for a different answer this time. "Zara, when you were a wee girl and you lived near Dunlyre, did you ever see the merfolk?"

Zara shook her head, sadness in her dark eyes. "No, I never did. Once I thought I heard them singing on the rocks, when I was kayaking with my father past the Grey Isle, but it was probably my imagination."

Taj slipped off Zara's knee and slithered on the floor, snapping his teeth. "Watch out! I'm a deadly killer eel!"

Sage stayed very still, her brain whirring. She knew the singing she'd heard wasn't in her imagination, because Finn had heard it too. And a cockle-shell box with a silver lock, just like the one Zara described, was hidden under her pillow.

Clambering to her feet, she grimaced at the pain in her ankles. She'd need to find that little pot of arnica. "Taj, quit that! Great story, Zara. I'm off to have a shower."

She limped off to get her washbag, thoughts still whirling.

If this story isn't just a folktale, if it all actually happened, and Finn and I have heard the merfolk singing, what does that mean? What on earth is going on?

8

FINN

When Finn woke, the weather had changed yet again. Sleet was pattering off the skylight, forming splashy wet circles on the glass. It reminded him of the sea, and of the swimmers yesterday. The girl's words echoed in his head: "Dolphins can stay underwater for about twenty minutes, so maybe it's the same for the merfolk."

Those guys weren't dolphins, I'm sure of it… So could they have been merfolk? But that's impossible, cos merfolk aren't real. Maybe I imagined it all…

But it didn't matter how hard he tried to persuade himself. Seeing those fishtailed swimmers dive was lodged in his brain. And as he lay on his back, warm under the duvet, his determination to get to the bottom of the mystery grew.

There has to be a rational explanation for all this, there has to be…

Downstairs, 'Winter Wonderland' was blaring. When they'd been in a shopping centre last week, Dad had grumbled about the festive tunes and complained that Lizzy had also been playing Christmas songs non-stop since mid-November. It was hard to believe that kind of behaviour wasn't annoying enough to make Dad pack his bags and leave her.

Last night, Finn had apologised to Lizzy as soon as he'd come back to the house. Doing it straightaway had been the less excruciating option; he knew his dad would make him say sorry eventually. Even when Lizzy had put her hands on his shoulders, looked into his eyes and said, "I understand, I really do," in a voice so sickly sweet he'd nearly puked on her shoes, he hadn't snarled, hadn't told her to back off. He'd thought about other things: Sage, and their plan to meet up, and the excellent excuse he'd need to invent to make that happen.

Rolling over, Finn glanced at his phone and was startled to see that it was almost ten o'clock. Throwing off the duvet, he dressed quickly, shoved a towel and goggles into his rucksack, and hurried downstairs. Yesterday's snow had vanished, and the back garden, with its soggy lawn and dead plants, had lost its magic. To the front, however, the huge grey sea with its frothy waves and distant, mist-shrouded islands promised adventure. The sleet had stopped falling, but the sky was dark, threatening more.

"Morning, sleepyhead!" Lizzy smiled at him as she buttoned Ava's coat.

She can do that herself. Don't treat her like a baby. And don't speak to me like I'm your kid. I know what you really think of me. You haven't even tried to deny it.

But he bit his lip and said nothing, just opened the fridge, found a carton of orange juice and tipped it into a glass. That was a concession too. At home, he'd have drunk straight from the carton.

"I'm taking Ava to Culzean Castle to see Santa Claus," announced Lizzy, pulling on her boots. "You can come too, if you like."

Ava cheered and flung her arms in the air, almost smacking Lizzy on the nose. "Santa's going to give me a present! And I'm going to give him my list." She ran over to Finn and handed him a piece of paper. The list was written in red crayon and the spelling was dire. Ava pointed to the bottom of the list, where she'd added items in pencil, under 'Litsaber' and 'Batmoabeel'.

"I've put two more things," she explained. "But one of them is only little, so there'll be plenty room in Santa's sack. I want a glittery hairband and a real unicorn. A flying one."

"Ava, unicorns can't fly." Finn didn't know much about unicorns, but he knew that.

"And Santa doesn't do live animals." Lizzy's voice was firm. "They're a definite no-no. Not fair to the animals, with the long flight and the chimney business." She walked towards Finn, that fake smile plastered on her face. "As I said, you're very welcome to come, Finn, but your dad thought you might prefer to go to the harbour cafe with him for an early lunch. Then he's meeting Duncan McPherson here to discuss the development."

Bet I'm as welcome as a nosebleed in that meeting. And nice one, Dad! Is your meeting really more important than taking your own kid to see Santa? And what's this about lunch? I haven't even had breakfast yet.

But the tiny cogs in his brain had started whirring. With Ava and Lizzy out of the picture and Dad busy, he might not even need an excuse to meet up with Sage this afternoon.

His dad looked up from the book he was reading. "Yeah, come with me, Finn. I thought we could take out the Wayfarer for a quick sail, then grab lunch."

Finn grinned, genuinely delighted. "Sure. That would be good. But I'm starving right now, so breakfast first."

After waving goodbye to Ava, and while his dad got organised for their sail, Finn prepared a light breakfast: cereal, toast and jam, and two blueberry muffins. He ate it standing at the front window, staring out to sea, excitement bubbling in his stomach.

Maybe we'll see those swimmers from the boat. If Dad sees them, then I'll know for sure I've not been imagining stuff. But… if they are real… what happens then?

Dad didn't say much as he drove down the steep, winding road to the harbour. With the Wayfarer on the trailer, he had to concentrate hard. Finn was impatient to set off, but they had to go through all the usual preparations: checking the equipment, compass, flares and first-aid kit, putting on wetsuits and life vests, and working together to rig the jib and the mainsail. It was only once they'd pushed off from the stone slipway that Finn remembered why he'd been so keen to go sailing in the first place.

As they scudded out to sea, the sails billowed, the Wayfarer heeled and salt spray blew in Finn's face. It was so exhilarating he laughed, and when he looked at his father, he was grinning too. It felt good to be in his dad's company, just the two of them for a change, and Dad seemed to agree.

"It's been too long since we've done this, hasn't it? Let's head out past that islet. We might spot some seals." He grinned at Finn. "This part of the firth is like a ships' graveyard! There are lots of interesting wrecks on the seabed. Maybe, when you're a bit older, we could go scuba diving and take a look?"

Finn nodded and held tight to the mainsheet as waves splashed against the boat and the wind whistled past his ears.

He focused on following his father's shouted instructions, helping Dad to keep the Wayfarer on an even keel and sailing in the right direction. It felt quite restful to do as he was told for once, without any arguing or eye-rolling, though he figured it was just as well he and Dad only ever did short trips.

But as they headed past the islet, towards the centre of the firth, the wind direction changed and the Wayfarer became harder to control. Scudding waves spat spray across the bow and the mainsail flapped.

"Sorry son, I think we need to head back to shore, just to be on the safe side," his father called. "Going about!"

Dad pushed the tiller, the boom swung and Finn ducked, and tugged on the mainsheet, eyes scanning the sea, desperate to spot one of the mysterious swimmers. And there did seem to be something moving through the waves. He stared, heart jumping, hoping against hope it was the fishtailed swimmers, and that his dad would see them too.

But it wasn't them. This shadowy presence was far too big, even larger than an orca. A huge, dark shape was undulating beneath the surface.

Finn blinked and shook his head, trying to shake his brain into action.

Is it just the shadow of the clouds? Reflections? But it can't be. It just broke through the waves, I'm sure it did. Something's there. A whale? It's flaming massive. Much,

much bigger than the Wayfarer…

Fear slithered in Finn's stomach.

Jeez. What the heck *is that?*

"Dad!" he croaked. "What's that? Over there, can you see it?"

His father turned to look, but a wave rolled through and it was too late. "Whatever it was, it's not there now." He grinned. "A seal, maybe, popping up for a nosey."

Finn grabbed the binoculars from the boat's hatch, but Dad was right. There was nothing there.

"Finn, can you put those away and concentrate! We're heeling too much."

Dad manoeuvred the little boat back towards the harbour, while Finn pulled at the billowing sails, his mind reeling.

I really must have concussion. I'm seeing things. Yesterday I hallucinated fishtailed swimmers and today it's freaking sea monsters.

They tied up the Wayfarer, took down the rigging, then hauled the boat out of the water and back onto the trailer. They changed into jumpers and jeans. Then Finn stood at the harbour wall and stared at the churning waves.

When his father came over and put an arm round his shoulders, he tensed.

Dad, I'm hallucinating stuff that's not there… Am I losing my mind?

"Are you okay, pal? Not seasick, I hope."

"No, I'm fine. Just starving."

"Glad to hear it. Let's get lunch."

Inside the harbour cafe, the air was warm and muggy. They ordered sausage, beans and chips and chatted as they ate, about football, and Finn's favourite subjects at school, and films they wanted to see – anything but the tricky stuff about Lizzy, Mum, the divorce, the access visits, John… All that stuff remained unsaid and clogged the atmosphere, made it impossible for Finn to feel happy and relaxed, and made him wish again that he could turn back the clock to the days before Lizzy came along and ruined everything.

He was just polishing off his ice cream when his dad finally broached a tricky subject.

"Listen, son. About that phone call you overheard…"

Don't go there, Dad. Don't take her side.

Heat crept up Finn's neck. He felt his cheeks burning. "You didn't hear her. I did. Don't call me a liar."

"I'm not calling you any such thing, Finn. But Lizzy says…"

"Stop, Dad, please. I know what I heard." Finn put his head in his hands, refusing to look at his father.

His father sighed, and looked at his watch. "Finn, I've got to go. I've to meet McPherson at one o'clock, walk him round the harbour and up to the house, and he doesn't like people to be late. I'll leave the car and trailer here and pick them up later."

There was only one car in the main car park, an elegant Aston Martin, so it wasn't hard to find the young, dark-haired man standing next to it. As Finn and his dad approached, Duncan McPherson waved at them but continued to shout into his phone.

"Well, send another email! It's not ruddy rocket science, you eejit!"

Finn caught his father's eye and pulled a face. "You didn't mention he's a jerk," he whispered.

His dad was about to answer when Duncan ended the call.

"Right, Tom. Let's get cracking." His eyes flicked over Finn, and he laughed. "Babysitting today, are you? Right, your models looked great, but now that we're here in the actual place, tell me exactly how you intend to transform this bleak hellhole into a destination people with dosh will want to visit."

They walked to the harbour, his dad clutching the plans and talking non-stop, excitedly pointing out the features of the proposed marina. McPherson was making no attempt to hide that he didn't think much of Dunlyre Harbour in its current state.

Finn leant over the wall to let the spray soak his face and cool his rising irritation.

McPherson's a total bampot. Why's Dad sucking up to him?

And then he heard it, so faint it was hardly there: distant singing, blown in with the tide. The feelings of homesickness and anxiety that the song stirred were ones he preferred to keep buried, and at first he wanted to clamp his hands over his ears and shut the singing out. But then he felt a fizz of excitement, a surge of elation that made him feel he could achieve anything. He just had to take that first step.

Finn stood back from the wall.

I might be imagining monsters, but I'm not imagining the singing. Sage heard it too.

He scanned the beach, and gazed at the black rocks, jutting out of the water near the shore.

Nothing there. But sound travels. Could the singing be coming from further out? But it can't be from the middle of the sea… What about that little rocky islet out in the firth? It has to be! I could swim out now, before I meet Sage, and find out what's going on.

Behind him, McPherson was still talking.

"What a dump! And it's freezing. Take me up to your house and we'll get a coffee."

"Righto. Are you coming, son?"

Finn didn't give his doubts a chance to gather. "Dad, I'm going for a walk. I'll see you later, okay?"

His dad nodded, too busy answering Duncan

McPherson's stream of questions to pay much attention.

Finn set off, swinging his rucksack, the wetsuit rolled inside. The singing stopped, and without it his nerves began to twang like plucked guitar strings.

Dad's going to be raging if he finds out I went swimming on my own. Absolutely raging... And he'd be right. It's a stupid, dangerous thing to do. If I get hypothermia...

He shook his head, trying to banish the negative thoughts, trying to hold on to the warm glow of elation he'd felt moments earlier.

This swim's happening. I'll worry about consequences later. It's not as if Dad always tells me what's going on. It's not like he doesn't hide stuff from me.

A woman passed him, dragging a reluctant Labrador. She coaxed it, "Come on, Lulu! It's not even raining..." and Finn had to bite his lip to stop tears from nipping at his eyes, because she sounded just like his mum, trying to coax Ava into doing her reading homework, or having a bath, or virtually anything that didn't involve eating ice cream. The thought of spending the whole of Christmas Day without his mother around was hurting more than he'd imagined.

I'll be home on the 27th. We'll do Christmas all over again. Two for the price of one!

Mum had smiled brightly, but her chin had trembled, and he'd realised this was hard for her too, and had given her a hug, and told her he'd be fine, and he'd take good care of Ava. After all, none of this mess was Mum's fault. It was all Lizzy's. But he wished his mother wasn't so far away. He wished she was here, instead of Lizzy.

The route down from the castle was steep, muddy and treacherous and he was relieved to reach the beach without slipping. Once there, he sat on a rock, took off his thick jacket and boots, unzipped his rucksack and tugged on his wetsuit and swim socks, being ultra-careful not to rip the thin neoprene. In the swim hat and goggles he'd be unrecognisable from a distance. Even if his dad spotted him, there was no way he'd know it was his son in the sea.

As Finn stood up, anxiety fluttered like moths in his stomach. At least the wind had dropped and the sea was relatively calm, the breaking waves frothing bubbles rather than churning foam. He thought of the thing he'd seen from the boat, but dismissed it.

It's easy to imagine moving objects in rolling waves. Tourists are always claiming they've seen the Loch Ness Monster. I need to stop imagining scary stuff and stop stressing. With any luck I'll find out if the singing is coming from the islet, or spot the fishtailed swimmers, and have some actual evidence for when I see Sage later.

Wading through slimy strands of kelp, Finn took some long, deep breaths and walked into the sea, splashing water on his face and neck to help guard against the sudden shock of the cold. The shore quickly fell away to waist-deep water. He dipped his hands in first, remembering his father's warnings about taking it slowly, and the cold burned his skin. But his body wasn't cold and, courage growing, he slowly submerged. When he lowered his chin, the water nipped his face like nettles. A surge of adrenalin shot through him. Swimming a strong-armed front crawl, legs kicking, he headed away from the beach towards the small islet he and his dad had passed earlier. It looked a lot closer from the beach below the castle than from the harbour, and as Finn swam, his confidence grew. Cutting through the waves was as exhilarating as being in the Wayfarer, and he felt powerful, and almost happy.

But a few minutes later when he lifted his head, the rocky islet seemed further away than it had from the shore. Every time he glanced up, it seemed he'd covered no distance at all. But he kept going, determined to finish what he'd started, trying to ignore the niggling doubts, and Gran's irritated voice. *You're as thrawn as your dad, Finn Robertson. Both stubborn as mules.*

Finn wondered if she was right.

Am I being stubborn? Don't fancy drowning just cos I'm too pig-headed to stop. And let's face it, there's nothing to see here but sea. What if the answer isn't on the islet at all?

The biting cold was numbing his lips and nose, and the initial excitement had faded. Visibility through his goggles was poor.

And the weather was deteriorating. The wind was blowing harder, whipping the waves into a frenzy. The clouds broke and hail started pelting down. Pea-sized missiles zinged against the water's surface, stinging his face.

Finn flipped over and started to swim back towards the shore. It wasn't far and he knew he was strong enough to make it. He'd swum further with Dad, many times. But with the water getting more and more choppy, he couldn't see where he was going. He couldn't see a thing but waves and hail. Blinded, disorientated, he stopped swimming and treaded water, holding one arm up to protect his head, fear making his pulse race.

Can't see the shore. What if I go the wrong way?

A wave broke over his head, knocking him sideways. He gulped a mouthful of salt water, then threw it back up, his dad's words pounding in his head.

You know what can happen to people in freezing water, don't you? The shock makes them fight for breath and that's when they swallow water. They die of drowning before hypothermia gets them.

The wind had whisked the water to froth and the shore had completely vanished. Finn knew he was in terrible trouble. His arms thrashed, and a scream rose in his throat.

"Help! Help me!"

A bigger wave crashed over him, filling his mouth with water, and silencing his scream, as he was thrown backwards and forwards by the force of the waves. The sea was winning. He could feel himself losing strength. Another wave rolled over him, sucking his body underwater. Desperate to stay calm, Finn focused on taking gulping breaths between each wave, kicking his legs like pistons to keep himself afloat. He glanced down, trying to gauge the water's depth. Hardly visible in the churning sea, a grey-black tail thrashed. Terror surged through Finn as he recalled the massive thing he'd seen from the boat. In the murky depths he glimpsed another tail, flicking back and forth in the cloudy water. There was more than one sea-creature down there.

Sharks!

If he'd been thinking logically, he'd have remembered only harmless basking sharks swam in the cold waters of Scotland's west coast. But news items about Australian surfers killed by great whites flashed through his brain. Panicking, he gasped and swallowed more seawater, making his throat burn. Another wave crashed over his head and sucked him under. Limbs flailing, trying to orientate himself, he peered through his goggles.

Focus. Which way's up? Where's the bottom?

He didn't have a clue.

Heart racing, blood pounding in his head, he lost all sense, opened his mouth and screamed. Seawater surged down his throat. His lungs felt as if they were going to explode.

I'm drowning. I'm going to die.

A hand grabbed his and pulled hard. The sea swirled and bubbled, and Finn felt himself being tugged through the water. He tried to struggle, though the grip was firm and he was weak with terror and exhaustion. His vision was blurred and it was impossible to think clearly. But he knew who they were.

Seaweed brushed against Finn's face, and one of the figures spoke right next to his ear, in a strange voice like bubbling water. Something was placed in his palm, and he held the object tight. Above, he could see daylight. As he surfaced, choking and gasping for breath, his fear ebbed away, replaced by overwhelming relief that he wasn't going to die after all.

Then he heard another voice in the distance, calling his name.

9

SAGE

Taj complained every step of the long walk to school from Cliff Lodges. Yesterday's beautiful snowy landscape had vanished and the world was a miserable grey.

"I don't want to go to school, Sage. Nobody likes me."

"It isn't for long, Taj. It's only a half day till the holidays!" She glanced over and saw him kick a stone into the gutter. "Incidentally, the other kids would like you more if you joined in their games. You don't even try."

Taj shrugged. "What's the point?"

She didn't bother to argue. He was right. What exactly was the point of making friends when they'd be moving on soon?

The morning felt endless, but when Sage put on her coat to go home at lunchtime, her fingers brushed against the cockle shell in her pocket, and even though she didn't really believe in merfolk, in her imagination she was in her kayak, paddling through sun-dappled waves, surrounded by beautiful, golden-haired creatures, all splashing their sparkly-scaled, iridescent tails in delight, overwhelmed with gratitude that she'd returned their precious treasure.

By the time she'd run home, Taj racing at her side, gleeful about the start of the holidays, Sage's heart was pounding with excitement, although the sea was as dull a grey as the sky, nothing like the enchanting sunlit scene she'd imagined. She almost flung Taj at Kate, who'd already started painting the placards for tomorrow's demonstration about the harbour development.

"I'll help later. I need to go. I'm meeting a friend, called, um, Grace. Miss Parker is being a real Grinch. She's given us a project to work on together over the holidays about, um... seabirds, like gulls and stuff. We're going to sketch the seagulls and do some research in the library. It'll take hours and hours, I expect."

"Oh, that sounds fun! I'm glad you'll have company." When Kate smiled, her eyes shone. "If you need any help identifying the birds, I'll be happy to lend a hand."

Sage felt a surge of guilt, but the lie couldn't be helped. *Let's face it, telling the truth would be like walking into quicksand.* She'd sink deeper the more she struggled to explain herself.

But when it came to Finn, the truth *was* an option.

92

When she met up with him, she'd need to make a decision. Should she keep the shell box to herself and try and solve the mystery alone, or show him?

By the time Sage reached the castle she could hear the singing again, faint and windblown, as if it was coming from out at sea. Her pulse started racing and her nerves tingled with excitement. Her fingers itched to grip the kayak's paddles. She was eager to feel the wind whipping her hair and cold sea spray dashing against her face, keen to dig the blades into the water and power through the waves. Nothing beat the exhilaration of speeding through the water by the force of her own muscles.

When the clocks had changed in October she'd made up her mind not to take the kayak out again until spring. It was getting darker by the time school ended for the day and the weather was too unpredictable. But because of today's early finish she had the chance to go out in daylight, and she was desperate to have a proper look around. She had an hour before she was due to meet Finn.

I need to find out whether merfolk exist, and this is my chance. If they do, and this shell box is theirs, did they leave it on the beach for me to find? And if so, why? What do they want?

Sage scrambled down the hill, taking care not to lose her footing. The narrow cleft in the cliff wall was an excellent hiding place, but in the last two months it had become clogged by seagrass and dead bracken. Dragging out the kayak wasn't easy, particularly as she needed to be able to re-hide it later.

When she'd managed to free it, she brushed off the worst of the dirt with a clump of dried kelp and stood for a moment, stroking the smooth fibreglass, admiring the sky-blue paintwork and ignoring the multiple scratches on the hull. With its long sleek lines, the kayak was easy to manoeuvre in waves and fantastic fun to paddle. It was the perfect boat.

She took the flotation device from the front hatch and pulled it over her head. It was less bulky and less buoyant than a life jacket, but it made swimming much easier, and there was always a chance she'd capsize.

As she shoved the kayak across the rocks towards the water, she passed a pile of discarded clothes on a rock. And she recognised that bright-red jacket, those designer-label boots.

That lad has more money than sense, leaving his fancy clothes where anyone could nick them. And what does the eejit think he's doing, going swimming all by himself?

She looked down at the kayak and grimaced.

But if he's an eejit, so am I. I guess we're both trying to be first to solve the mystery.

Staring out to sea, trying to get a glimpse of Finn, she

spotted a black-clad head and arms swimming in the direction of the Grey Isle, the same place she was planning to go. If Zara's story was true and the merfolk lived on rocks, rather than in a magical undersea kingdom, they might be on the Grey Isle, well away from the harbour, the houses and people.

So we're both crazy, but at least I've got a boat.

She'd found the kayak in July, washed up on the rocks, the fibreglass hull badly damaged but watertight, and she had hauled it up to the base of the cliff as a kind deed, presuming the owner would come and take it away. But nobody had. It had lain there for days, getting pooped on by gulls and running the risk of being swept away at high tide. Eventually, Sage convinced herself that nobody wanted it, and it had become a case of finders keepers.

She'd hardly been able to believe her luck. The kayak even had a paddle clipped to the side. When she'd taken another look and found a spare folding paddle in the back hatch and a waterproof torch and whistle inside the front one, it had felt like Christmas. And when she'd put on the flotation device and it had fitted perfectly, it had seemed meant, as if she were Cinderella and the device was her glass slipper.

Zara was an experienced kayaker, and when they'd lived briefly in the Yorkshire Dales a couple of years ago, she'd often taken Sage out on the river, so Sage was already competent in paddling techniques and rolling skills. And it was a lot more fun in her own boat than it had been in borrowed kayaks.

For the first few weeks she'd stayed close to shore, but by September she'd dared herself to paddle out to the tiny islets, to watch fat seals sunning themselves on the rocks and red-billed oystercatchers prising open cockles. When she'd jumped out of the kayak and stood on the rocks, she'd felt like Robinson Crusoe. But she'd never gone as far as the Grey Isle.

Sage fumbled for the shell box, touched its ribbed surface. When she shook it, she heard the mysterious rustling sound. Even on a dull day like this, the little silver lock gleamed. She was sure the box belonged to merfolk. And they'd want it back. Anticipation fizzed like sherbet in her stomach.

Sage pulled off her boots and socks, abandoning them next to Finn's. In summer she'd worn a T-shirt over a swimsuit and had sneaked it into the rest of the washing in the communal laundry. Explaining sodden outer clothes would be a lot trickier. Her parents would have a fit if they knew what she was doing right now.

They'd be raging, and they'd be right to be angry. But I'm going.

She shoved the kayak across the rocks, utterly determined. She needed to have an adventure of her own, not one she

96

was being dragged on against her will by Kate and Zara. She wanted to experience something incredible, all by herself. She wanted to meet merfolk, escape into their world, leave real life behind for a while. Because she knew that when she started at a new school in Cornwall, when the teasing began and nobody wanted to be her friend because she didn't speak like they did or because her clothes were weird, she wouldn't care, because she would have a magical secret.

As Sage pushed the kayak into the shallows and straddled it, the burning cold in her feet sent a shiver running right up her spine. The waves were choppier than they'd looked from the shore and the wind was biting. Paddling the kayak wasn't the pleasant experience it had been in the summer; it was an endurance test, and she had to use all her strength and skills to keep the boat from rolling. But it was a thrill ride too, and adrenalin buzzed through her body.

Ahead of her, the Grey Isle looked as dreary as its name, but she hoped it was hiding magic in dull camouflage. As she headed into deeper water, she paddled harder, keeping her body upright, burying the blade into the waves, using her core muscles to power through the sea. She was closing in on Finn, who appeared to be an impressively confident and able swimmer.

She was wondering what on earth she should say to him as she paddled past, when the weather worsened and a sudden hailstorm began. Hailstones bounced off the kayak's body, cracking like gunshots. The waves tossed the little boat around, and Sage was struggling both to keep it upright and to see which way to go. Fear knotted her stomach.

Then, without warning, a wave hit the kayak side-on. As her boat tipped, Sage didn't hesitate. She'd practised a low brace many, many times. Placing the back of the blade on the surface, she leant her upper body towards it and struck the water with the flat paddle, using her hips to right the kayak. As soon as the boat was balanced, she sat upright and scanned the waves, struggling to see through the pelting hailstones. The satisfaction she'd felt at saving herself from capsizing dissolved.

Where's Finn? He was over there a second ago. Where has he gone?

When she yelled his name, the wind grabbed her voice and tossed it like waste paper. And then, as suddenly as it had started, the hailstorm stopped. Desperately, Sage stared at the churning sea and her heart plummeted. Finn had gone under. Panic swept over her and her voice was a hoarse screech.

"Finn! Where are you?"

A whistle was attached to the flotation device, but would anyone hear it? There was an emergency flare in the hatch too, but the lifeboat station was in Ayr. How long would it take for help to arrive?

She shoved the paddle deep into the cockpit, allowing the boat to bob aimlessly, and fumbled with frozen fingers for the whistle, her eyes still on the water, desperately seeking any sign: a waving hand, a bobbing head… But there was nothing.

The whistle was pressed to her lips when, with a sudden upswell of water, Finn's body surfaced, the wetsuit gloss-black as sealskin. He appeared to be floating on his back, and she couldn't be sure if he was alive or dead. Dropping the whistle, she grabbed the paddle and headed in his direction, shouting his name.

An undercurrent of fear dragged at her, making paddling hard. There was something wrong about the position of Finn's body. His head was back, his arms limp. It was as if he was being held up out of the water.

When she reached him, he turned his head and vomited up seawater. Relief flooded her body. His eyes were rolling, but he was trying to speak. Then, as if he had been tossed by a powerful wave, his body rose out of the water and tumbled across the front of the kayak, making the little boat lurch. Frantic, Sage dug in and, astonishingly, the kayak didn't capsize.

She yelled at the boy, not knowing if he was in any condition to hear. "Hold on to the straps and I'll get you home!"

The fingers of Finn's right hand spread like tentacles

and clung to the elastic straps that latticed the front of the kayak. But his left hand remained in a tight fist, and his legs dangled in the water. He was white as a ghost, his lips bluish-grey. As Sage got ready to battle the waves, she glanced to the side and jumped with fright.

Just below the surface of the water she could see two large, round eyes staring up at her. A narrow face. Long hair drifting like seaweed.

Sage stared back, her heart banging against her ribs. She felt giddy with amazement, buzzing with triumph.

"Oh jeez… Look… They're real," she whispered, wishing with all her heart she could share this moment. "Zara, Taj, we were right… Merfolk are real!"

The waves rippled, as if the creature was moving, and Sage remembered the shell box.

"Wait!" She fumbled for the shell, but her hands were numb with cold and in this sitting position the flotation device was covering her pocket. "I've got your treasure! Wait!"

But the face sank out of sight, far beneath the waves.

For a second she gazed around, waiting for the creature to surface, but there was only a tiny splash. Finn's left arm had slipped into the water.

"Hold on! I'm taking you home! You'll be okay."

Giving herself a shake, Sage started to paddle back to shore.

The return journey was strange. She'd thought having Finn's body draped over the front would make the kayak near-impossible to manoeuvre and very likely to roll, but the boat seemed to be motorised, it sped so quickly through the waves. It was almost as if it was being pushed from behind, but when she glanced round, she couldn't see anything there.

By the time they reached the beach, Finn had vomited up more seawater and seemed to be recovering. Sage helped him to a rock and found a large towel in his bag, which she draped over his shoulders. As she hauled the kayak back into its cave, she felt a tinge of worry and hoped the boy wasn't watching. She didn't feel ready to share its hiding place.

When she returned, Finn was sitting, shoulders hunched, his expensive jacket on, hood up, a warm fleece hat over his still-damp hair and a dazed expression in his eyes. He was shivering, and she wished she could light a fire to warm him up.

"Did you see them?" he whispered. "The merfolk?"

She nodded, relieved and thrilled that he'd seen them too. "I saw one. A face under the water. It was amazing. The most incredible thing that's ever happened to me. Merfolk exist! Isn't it brilliant!"

"Yeah, though they gave me a real fright. I thought I was being attacked by sharks. But the merfolk saved my life."

His voice was uncertain, as if he was struggling to believe what had happened. "I was drowning, and they lifted me, like I was weightless. Thank you, by the way, for getting me back to shore." He paused, and chewed on his lip. "I've been thinking… can I leave my wetsuit and towel to dry in that cave with your kayak?"

Sage didn't reply. He'd seen her hide the boat after all then.

"Please, Sage. I doubt my dad will notice they're missing, but he'll definitely notice if I carry them back to the house soaking wet, and I can't face the aggro."

She couldn't help but notice the bitter tinge in his voice. Finn seemed to have a lot of worries already, and it seemed mean to add another.

"Sure. You can lay them over the kayak, so they dry properly."

She even helped him do it, holding back the curtain of foliage. When he'd finished, he turned to her, his expression serious. The colour was beginning to return to his cheeks and his lips had lost that awful blue tinge. In fact, he seemed to be recovering remarkably quickly.

"I really am grateful, you know. If you hadn't been out there, I'd have been in serious trouble, even after the merfolk brought me up to the surface. I don't think I'd have made it."

"Are you sure you're okay now?" Sage pointed at Finn's tightly clamped fist. "Is your hand alright?"

Finn nodded. "Yeah, it's fine. I'm just holding tight to this, in case I drop it. When they grabbed hold of me, one of them put it in my hand. What do you think it is?"

Slowly, he uncurled his fist. A tiny silver object, curved like a seahorse, glinted in the palm of his left hand. Even on a dull winter's afternoon, even though the light was beginning to fade, the tiny object seemed to shimmer with magic.

A ripple of excitement ran through Sage. She knew what this was. Picking it up and holding it between her thumb and forefinger, she used her other hand to rummage in her pocket and bring out the shell.

"They must want us to open this box," she whispered, "because they've given you the key."

10

FINN

As he examined the object Sage had taken from her pocket, Finn shivered, though whether it was with excitement or cold, he couldn't tell. At first glance it looked like an ordinary cockle shell and he was less than impressed, but as soon as it was in his hands, he could see it was special. That lock hadn't been glued on; it had been expertly set into the shell where the two halves met. Sage was right: it was a box, and he'd just been given the key.

He closed his eyes, remembering the weird, bubbling voice from under the sea. But now, the words made sense.

"I know it'll sound mad, but one of the merfolk spoke to me, underwater. He said:

"You heard us sing, and so did she.
She has the box. You hold the key."

Finn handed the shell box back. "So, did the merfolk give this to you?"

"No, I found it, here, on the rocks, yesterday," Sage explained. "I think perhaps they left it for me to find, though I don't know why."

"Well, we'd better open it. Do you think there's treasure in it? A massive pearl or something?"

Sage shook her head. "Nope. It rustles. Listen!" She shook it beside his ear. "Hey, you're shivering. We need to get you warmed up. Let's go to the cafe and buy a hot chocolate." Her hands drifted to her pockets, and her face flushed. "Oh, I forgot. I didn't bring any cash. Look, maybe you should go home and have a hot shower. Don't want you getting ill."

"I feel fine, weirdly fine! And I've got money." He felt in his pockets. "Yup, still here. I'll get you a hot chocolate too, as a thanks for saving my life. Whipped cream and marshmallows optional but recommended. We can open the shell box in the cafe, in the warmth."

A smile lit up Sage's face. "Okay. Thanks! I guess that's fair."

Stepping into the cafe, a blast of warm air hit Finn in the face. It felt like heaven. After ordering the drinks, he peeled off his jacket and hat, and huddled close to the radiator, letting the heat soak into his chilled bones.

"I had lunch here with my dad," he told Sage. "Seems like ages ago, but it was just a couple of hours. My head's spinning with everything that's just happened."

"Me too! It's mad, isn't it?" Excitement shone in her eyes and she gripped the sides of her seat, as if to stop herself bouncing like Tigger. It was nice to see, as Sage seemed so super-serious and sensible, as though she spent all her time around adults instead of other twelve-year-olds. "I mean, I know you nearly drowned, and that must have been horrible, but I can't believe we just saw actual merfolk!"

"I didn't really see them." Finn tried to think back to those desperate minutes below the surface. "I was past seeing anything. But they rescued me. I felt them grab my wrist and pull me up, I knew it was them."

I was an absolute numpty, going swimming alone. I totally nearly drowned out there. What if I'd died and they didn't find my body for weeks? How grim would that have been for Dad and Mum and poor wee Ava?

The thought of Ava's distress made him feel quite sick.

She's so excited about Christmas. I'd have ruined everything for her, if I'd got myself killed. And it wouldn't have been great for me either. Dead people don't get presents.

Sage was watching his face, and she looked worried now. "Finn, are you sure you're okay?"

"It's weird. I honestly thought I was going to die out there, but now I feel fine, almost like it never happened. I mean, I feel like an idiot for going out on my own. But I'm okay." He tried to think of a logical explanation, but failed. "It's kind of spooky really."

He stopped talking because the waitress arrived to plonk two mugs on the table. The hot chocolate, topped with frothy whipped cream and fluffy pink marshmallows, was completely delicious. They were the cafe's only customers, and as soon as she'd served them, the waitress scuttled back into the kitchen.

While they sipped, Sage told him about the legend of the merfolk she'd heard from her mother. To Finn, it sounded as plausible as the Loch Ness Monster guff that got trotted out for tourists. But logic didn't seem to apply here. Real life and story were blending like a river meeting the sea.

When Sage finished her story, he told her about seeing the fishtailed swimmers through the harbour telescope. And how yesterday that had seemed too crazy to say out loud.

Sage grinned. "Might be a good idea to keep it quiet. It'll seem pretty crazy to most people."

"Hey, I'm not the weird kid who's carrying a shell around in my pocket and insisting it belongs to the merfolk."

Sage burst out laughing and he joined in, pleased to have made her laugh. She looked less like a mini adult.

"Speaking of the shell box…" Carefully, Sage placed it on the table between them.

Finn uncurled his fist and they both stared at the tiny, delicate silver key.

His heart was knocking against his ribs and his fingers felt stiff and clumsy as he inserted the key in the lock. He slid the box closer to Sage.

"You found it. You should open it."

She didn't argue, and her hands trembled with excitement as she picked it up and gently turned the key. With a sharp click the hinged lid sprang open, exposing the shell's beautiful, iridescent interior, a gleaming swirl of sea-blues and ocean-greens. And in the centre…

Sage sighed. "Well, that's a bit of a let-down."

"What the heck is that? A Brussels sprout?" Finn couldn't keep the disappointment out of his voice. He examined the lump inside the shell. It wasn't a sprout but a tightly wrapped ball of what appeared to be seaweed. He passed it to Sage, whose bemused expression mirrored his own, saying, "It's sushi. Better than sprouts. They're minging."

She laughed and wrinkled her nose. "Gotta say, I was hoping for something more exciting."

Holding the little ball close to her face, she tried to peel the thin layers gently apart, but it was no use. "It's kelp, I think, and it's bone-dry. That's why it was making that rustling sound." She chewed on her lip, thinking. "Maybe it'll uncurl if we soak it in water."

She asked the waitress for a glass of warm tap water. The girl rolled her eyes, but handed one over and returned to the kitchen.

"Will we give it a go?" Sage whispered, holding the seaweed ball over the glass.

Finn nodded, leaning forward.

When the ball hit the water, it floated, a dull, grey-green sprout. A couple of minutes ticked by and it looked like nothing was going to happen at all. He felt his shoulders slump as disappointment settled.

Then a tiny, iridescent bubble formed on the ball, floated lazily to the surface and popped. Another followed, and another, until thousands of tiny bubbles were fizzing, turning still water into sparkling. As the bubbles swirled and popped, the water began to froth, lapping against the sides of the glass like miniature waves, its colour transformed from clear to a luminous emerald. As the children watched, the ball began to slowly unravel and expand, like a conjuror's trick, until a glossy green frond filled the glass.

Finn stuck his fingers in the water, pulled out the dripping strand of kelp and laid it on the table.

"Wow. That was pretty impressive." He poked the strand with his finger. "But it's still just seaweed."

Sage leaned in and flipped it over. "When you lifted it out, I thought I saw... Yeah, I was right... Look at the marks."

Finn stared. The other side of the frond was etched with dark lines and squiggles. "What's it meant to be?"

Sage held it in both hands and examined it carefully, but her expression remained baffled. The silence was only broken by the waitress clattering crockery in the kitchen. Laying the frond back down on the table, Sage shrugged. "No clue."

Finn leaned back in his chair, feeling weary. Then his eyes fell on a map of Dunlyre and its coastline pinned to the cafe wall. He looked down at the frond, traced the longest curve with his finger and started to speak at exactly the same time as Sage.

"I think it's a map of this area. See—"

"It's a map of this coastline, isn't it?" Excitement danced in her eyes. "Look, that curve's the harbour and that splodge there is the Grey Isle."

He checked with the poster on the wall. "Yeah, and that rectangle's the castle. It's a map alright. But why would the merfolk give us a map?"

Sage sipped her hot chocolate, her face thoughtful. "Remember what they said to you? They sang, and we heard them, so they've given this to us. They've planned this: they want us to find them!"

As her words tumbled over each other, he could imagine meeting the merfolk, swimming with them, learning to dive as confidently as they did, impressing his dad with his newfound skills.

Is this real? Am I really thinking about a swim meet with merfolk?

"Even if you're right, Sage, we still don't know where to look. This map isn't much help, is it?"

Together they stared at the markings — the strange squiggles and the long line of curves. Using one finger Finn followed the long line that marked the bays and coves on the coastline, and then noticed something so tiny he hadn't spotted it immediately.

"See this mark here, like a 'w'? I think that's meant to be a fishtail. I think that could be where they are."

Sage's voice wobbled with excitement. "Oh, wow! I can't be definite, but I'm pretty sure that's Whin Bay. It's a rocky cove, and you can't reach it from land — unless you abseil down the cliff. It's not very special-looking; I've passed it a few times in the kayak, and it didn't seem worthwhile stopping. But maybe that's where we'll find them." She looked at him, eyes shining. "I'm going to explore the cove tomorrow. I'll understand if you don't want to get back in the water. But I'm going to take the kayak out first thing in the morning."

Finn's phone buzzed: a message from Dad. He stood up and put his jacket and hat on.

"I need to go. But I want to come tomorrow, so I'll meet you at the castle?"

Carefully, Sage rolled up the map, closed it back in the shell box and stuffed that in her pocket. "Are you sure? I don't think I'd want to go swimming again the next day if I'd almost drowned."

"I'm fine, honestly."

She nodded. "It'll be properly light by half eight. We'll stick close to shore. For safety's sake. Okay?"

"Okay, pal." He lowered his voice as the waitress arrived to collect the mugs. "Tomorrow we'll go to Whin Bay. Avoid drowning. Meet a whole pod of merfokes."

She grinned, eyes shining. "Just one would be amazing. See you tomorrow, Finn."

11

FINN

When Finn reached the holiday house, he saw his father slumped on the wooden bench in the front garden. His dad was staring out to sea, a troubled expression on his face, oblivious to the darkening sky and the icy wind.

Wonder what's up with Dad? Did his meeting go badly? Bet he won't tell me if it did.

A small voice in his brain reminded him that his dad had tried to talk to him, but he'd shut him down... twice in the last two days.

Finn flung himself onto the bench beside his father. "Hiya. Did your meeting with Mr McPherson go okay?"

His dad jumped, clearly so deep in thought he hadn't even noticed Finn's arrival, and then gave him a rueful smile. "Yeah, it was fine. Sorry it took a while. Hope you weren't too bored. Can't have taken you long to walk around this wee place!

Maybe you should have gone to see Santa after all, eh?"

"No way. I'm happy to wait until the 25th. Anyway, I had a good time. I went for a walk along the beach."

His dad raised an eyebrow. "Really? What did you do? Rockpooling? Stone skimming?" His face brightened. "We could have a competition if you like. I was stone-skimming champion in my day."

"No, I didn't skim stones. I—" Finn hesitated. He could hardly tell his dad he'd gone swimming and been saved by merfolk. After the massive row he'd get for going into the water alone, he could just imagine the conversation about the merfolk.

"Dad, I was rescued by merfolk."

"What are you on about, Finn? What on earth are merfolk?"

"They're mythical creatures. See, I met this girl. Her name's Sage, she's really nice, and anyway, Sage and I think merfolk live on the rocks round here."

"Right… Wait a minute, son. You got a bang on the head the other night, didn't you? I think you might have delayed concussion. We'll need to get you to the docs…"

An awkward silence had fallen. Finn and his father sat side by side on the bench, not touching. The sky was grey-black, mirrored by the sea. Far below them, the harbour lights had been switched on. It was getting dark.

I should say something. Something that'll make things like they used to be, before…

But he could think of nothing he could bear to say out loud, and anyway his stomach was rumbling. "Are we going out for dinner?"

His dad laughed. "We went out for lunch! I'm not made of money, kid. Anyway, we've got a dinner guest. McPherson invited himself. He's coming back later."

Finn pulled a face. "Great."

"I sense you're as enthusiastic about the prospect as I am. He is hard work, isn't he? I'll be glad to get this commission done and dusted." Finn waited, wondering if his dad would say more, but he didn't. Instead, he jumped up, and pulled Finn to his feet. "Right, let's head inside. I've already broken the bad news about McPherson joining us to Lizzy, and she wasn't too thrilled."

In the house, Ava was bouncy as a wallaby and rosy-cheeked with excitement. "We saw the real Santa, Finn! He had a real white beard! He let me pull it really hard and it didn't come off!"

"She didn't half pull hard. The poor old man had tears in his eyes." Lizzy shuddered at the memory and poured herself a large glass of wine. "Why don't you run upstairs, Ava, sweetheart, and get the lovely present Santa gave you?"

"Can I have a glass of wine too, love? It's been tough going this afternoon, and it's not over yet. I need some relaxation time." Finn's father gave a martyred sigh and threw himself on the couch, shoving a cushion under his head. If there had been a telly, Finn guessed he'd be reaching for the remote right now. Sometimes his dad really didn't get the vibes.

Lizzy's eyebrow shot up. "Um, I don't think so! The oven's over here, Tom. I bought some macaroni and tinned tuna. You can make a nice tuna pasta bake for dinner, and pour yourself some wine while you're at it."

Ignoring his protests, Finn hauled his father off the couch and pushed him towards the kitchen. Lizzy might be the enemy, but Mum would be horrified if she knew he'd let his dad get away with behaviour like that. Gran would have been chasing Dad round the kitchen, brandishing her handbag. And, more importantly, he was starving and his dad's tuna pasta bake was amazing.

"You might imagine your afternoon has been tough, but I've spent mine visiting Santa with an over-excited five year-old." Lizzy dropped the tin of tuna into Dad's hands.

Finn smirked at him. "Yeah, Dad. Get cooking. Don't forget to add boiled eggs. Mr McPherson will love it."

Ava hurtled downstairs, clutching a Spider-Man figure. "Look at my toy! It has a real web shooter." She handed the action figure to Finn.

"Nice. I might have a motorbike for him in a box at home. I'll look it out for you."

Ava grinned, delighted. "Santa said I couldn't have a Spider-Man toy, because they were in the boy's pile, but Lizzy told him he was a 'seck-sist git'. She gave Santa a big row!"

Dad groaned. "Oh, Lizzy, you did not! Wait until you meet Duncan McPherson. Sparks are going to fly."

Lizzy pulled a face and took a large slug of wine. "Why, is McPherson a sexist git too?"

Despite himself, Finn felt a smile flicker. It looked as though this evening could get interesting.

He started to head upstairs, but Lizzy stood in his way. "And you can help too, Finn. Lay the table, please. There are place mats in that drawer."

Finn sighed, but he went to fetch the mats.

By the time McPherson arrived, thirty minutes late, their stomachs were rumbling. Throwing his overcoat down on the couch, he stood in the middle of the room, hands on his hips, smiling that attractive dimpled grin. He looked rather like Prince Eric in the *Little Mermaid* movie, and Finn noticed Ava watching him with interest.

"Excellent, Tom. Nice little place you've got here! And what a beautiful wife!"

"Give me strength," muttered Lizzy. "How lovely to meet you at last!" she added in a louder voice.

When McPherson walked towards the kitchen area,

where Dad was busy taking the pasta bake out of the oven, Ava followed. "'Scuse me, Mr Ferson. 'Scuse me."

He ignored her, so she tugged hard at the back of his jacket.

McPherson spun round. "Oi! This jacket's Paul Smith, I'll have you know."

Ava gazed at him, eyes wide. "Shouldn't you give it back to him? You shouldn't steal other people's clothes."

Lizzy put her hand on Ava's shoulders. "Was there something you wanted to say to Mr McPherson?"

"I just wanted to ask… I wanted to know if he was like Santa."

McPherson laughed. "I'm afraid I haven't brought any presents!"

Ava shook her head. "No, I meant, are you a seck-sist git, like Santa?"

"Ava!" Dad paled, and Lizzy's hands flew to her face. Finn had to fight so hard not to laugh he thought he might implode.

McPherson ran a hand through his abundant hair. "Perhaps it's time for the kiddies to get off to bed?"

"No way." Ava glowered. "I'm starving with hunger." She turned to Finn and added in a stage whisper. "Cos Mr Ferson was late for dinner."

"Look, Duncan, why don't you sit down at the table?" Lizzy pulled out a chair. "Tom's made a lovely pasta bake."

The pasta bake was a little overdone, which wasn't his dad's fault, and the conversation became increasingly awkward, which *was* his dad's fault, because he brought up the subject of the harbour development.

"We're all ready for the big meeting at the end of the week," he said, taking a swig of red wine. "Hopefully our plans will go through without any problems."

McPherson nodded. "Let's hope so. I've got a news crew organised at the harbour tomorrow. By the way, I was thinking that in future we could convert that wrecked castle into a hotel."

Lizzy coughed, and Finn wondered at first if she'd choked on one of the crunchy pieces of pasta. "It's a medieval castle, Mr McPherson!" There was real horror in her voice. "That 'wreck' is steeped in history."

"It might be ancient, but it's a still a wreck." McPherson waved a hand, dismissing Lizzy. Finn noticed her eyes narrow and heard her hiss "Philistine!" under her breath. He didn't know what it meant, but it sounded rude.

Ava, whose eyes had glazed over with boredom, sat up straighter in her chair and tugged Finn's sleeve. "What's a Filis-thingy? Is it the same as a seck-sist git?"

Finn put a warning finger to his lips and, oblivious, McPherson continued. "I was thinking about the harbour development. Speedboats, and jet-skis for the youngsters, will be a big draw. We really need to push for those."

His dad smiled. "We've been jet-skiing, haven't we, Finn? We had a fantastic time."

Finn nodded. He'd loved whizzing about on the water, but that was before… There was a programme on TV last month about the injuries caused to the manatees in Florida by speedboats and jet-skis. The merfolk could get hurt. He opened his mouth to tell Mr McPherson about the programme, then closed it.

What's the point? There are no manatees round here, and I can hardly mention the flipping merfolk.

Lizzy's cutlery clattered as she set it down. "Mr McPherson, jet-skis here would be totally inappropriate." Her voice was chilly. "Personally, I think this quiet, peaceful seaside village, with its pretty harbour and magnificent castle, is perfect just as it is."

Finn's dad gulped and reached for the wine bottle, but his aim was off. The bottle toppled, red wine splashed across the table, and bright crimson droplets splattered over McPherson's snow-white shirt.

His dad gave a horrified gasp. "Oh, I'm so sorry!"

Finn stuffed his fist into his mouth, trying in vain to stop a snort of laughter escaping, while Ava burst into hiccupping giggles.

"This shirt cost a fortune," growled McPherson, wiping at his chest with a paper napkin.

Lizzy caught Finn's eye, and winked, but he looked away.

We both think McPherson's a bampot. It doesn't make us pals.

"Oh dear. What a dreadful shame, Mr McPherson." Lizzy stood up and started gathering the plates. "Perhaps you should head back to your hotel and rinse your shirt in the sink. I'd lend you one of Tom's, but I'm not sure it would fit. You're so much taller. Your coat's still on the back of the couch. If you button it up, nobody will notice the state you're in."

On his way out, McPherson patted Ava on the head and she growled like a Rottweiler. McPherson pulled his hand away, alarm on his face.

Dad saw him out to the car and came back, his face drawn, eyes red with tiredness. "Well that was a catalogue of disasters," he sighed. "First Ava calls my client a sexist git, then my wife tells him his harbour development is going to be an environmental disaster for the area, and then I top it off by spilling wine all down his front... Oh yes, and my son laughs about it. If I'm not turfed off this commission, it'll be a miracle."

"If you are, it'll be a good thing," retorted Lizzy as she led Ava upstairs to get ready for bed. "That man is ghastly and I'd much rather you weren't doing business with him."

Finn flopped onto the couch.

It feels very weird to be on the same side as someone I can't stand. Think my head's about to explode...

Even though he felt weirdly okay for someone who'd almost drowned, it had been a long, tiring day. As his head sank into the soft cushions, he closed his eyes.

"Think you need an early night, son. You look shattered."

Finn didn't argue, just dragged himself upstairs and got undressed. Before he went to sleep, he googled 'Cianalas'. Nothing much came up, other than it was Gaelic for homesickness. But when he googled 'Tsunami Britain', it turned out that the first part of Sage's merfolk story was kind of true. At the end of the Ice Age, a massive landmass known as Doggerland had been one of the richest hunting and fishing grounds in Europe, until the sea rose too far and claimed it all. Finn tried to imagine what it must feel like to be swamped by a giant, unstoppable wall of water.

Maybe we'd have time to get in the Wayfarer and ride the wave...

He couldn't find any information about Ice Age tsunami survivors who evolved into merfolk and travelled round the coast to the Firth of Clyde. Merfolk, according to Google, were mythical creatures.

Turns out Google doesn't know everything.

Exhausted, Finn closed his computer, lay down and shut his eyes. Immediately, images of being knocked underwater by churning waves began flashing through his brain. All over again he felt the awful burning sensation in his lungs, the terrible fear that he was drowning, and the gut-wrenching terror when he'd seen those thrashing fishtails. And then the relief as arms reached for him and lifted him to the surface.

The merfolk existed. He'd seen them. Sage had seen them. And they'd given her the shell box and given him the key. They'd wanted him and Sage to find the map. The merfolk wanted to be found. And tomorrow morning, he and Sage were going to Whin Bay to look for them.

12

SAGE

"Hi, guys. Charlotte's laid us an egg for Christmas!"

When Sage walked into the cabin with the warm, newly laid egg clutched in her gloved hand, she was hit by a blast of heat and a rich herbal smell. It felt good to be home, and the thrill of what she'd seen was buzzing inside her.

In the morning, I'm going to do the most exciting thing I've ever done. I'm going with Finn to find the merfolk. They're waiting for us, I know it. I just wish I knew why...

As she closed the door she noticed Zara tuck away the long, striped scarf she'd been knitting. Sage guessed it was her Christmas present. She'd have to practise a delighted face for when she unwrapped it. She'd have to pretend she didn't mind that it wasn't a mobile phone or a gift card. She fully appreciated that using charity shops and recycling hand-me-downs and making your own clothes was sensible and ethical, but she longed, just once, to be able to walk into a store and buy some new clothes with the same labels the other girls wore.

She gave the egg to Kate, who was busy in the kitchen, cooking dinner. Taj was by the fire, building an impressive structure from wooden blocks.

"Come and look at my castle, Sage. And this blue sparkly material, that's the sea."

She knelt down to admire the castle. "It's brilliant, Taj. That must be the way Dunlyre Castle looked in the olden days, before it got wrecked." She pointed at the small plastic figure lying on the cloth. "What's Batman up to?"

"He's not being Batman. He's being the merfolk, swimming in the sea, like the ones I saw." He put his finger to his lips, sharing a secret, and this time she didn't argue.

"Have you and your schoolfriend been working on the seabird project all afternoon?" asked Kate. "I'd love to have a look when it's finished!"

Sage gulped. There was no chance of that happening. "Yeah. Me and Grace spent ages drawing seagulls. It's tricky, because the blooming things won't stay still, and we had to run for shelter when the hail started. Grace is keeping all our work safe in her room. She doesn't share with a wee brother."

And she isn't my friend. Grace McNiven hardly knows I exist.

She'd said hi to Grace when she and Taj had arrived at school in the morning, but Grace had been too busy chatting to her cousin Mia about their plans for Christmas and hadn't even bothered to look in Sage's direction. Mia was going on a skiing holiday, apparently, and Grace was staying at their gran's. Neither girl had asked Sage what she was doing, because they couldn't care less. Sage had stuck her chin in the air, determined not to care either, but she *had* cared, and right now the lies felt sour on her tongue. Still, the truth was impossible.

Zara gave Sage a hopeful smile. "I'm so pleased you've made friends at school."

"Just one pal, but yeah, Grace is nice."

Liar. She's not one bit nice, at least not to me. But it's not a total fib. I've got a friend now... Finn. So I've just changed some details.

Luckily, her parents didn't ask for those.

"Can you set the table, love?" called Kate. "Dinner's nearly ready."

Sage pushed aside all thoughts of the merfolk and helped to set the table. Before they ate, she took the present her teacher, Miss Parker, had given her out of her schoolbag and placed it under their little potted fir tree, so she'd have a surprise to open on Christmas morning. Taj's present from Mrs Ghauz, a polystyrene glider, had been unwrapped right away, and was already broken.

"So, how was school this morning?" asked Kate, as she heaped veggie lasagne onto Sage's plate.

'It was rubbish.' Taj stabbed at his dinner with his fork. "Die, lasagne!"

Zara frowned. "Taj, that's enough. And Kate was speaking to Sage, not you."

Sage chewed on a lump of garlic bread and considered her answer. Kate and Zara would have been appalled by the lack of educational input on the last morning of school. The children had gathered in the hall to sing Christmas songs and then they'd watched three quarters of a movie. Once they'd been herded back to their classroom, Miss Parker had let them make glittery decorations to take home. She hadn't been thrilled when Sage pointed out that glitter was very bad for the environment. At break time, Mrs Garrison, the school secretary and self-appointed Scrooge, had dismantled the Christmas tree in the foyer, grumbling, "I won't have time later, so it might as well be done now." It had all been a bit grim.

But it doesn't matter because there's so much other, more exciting stuff. I went out in the kayak, I helped to save a friend from drowning, we saw merfolk underwater, we opened a locked shell box and discovered a secret map.

"School was fine," she replied, keeping her eyes on her plate. "Your placards look great, by the way. I'll make mine after dinner."

Usually Sage enjoyed this sort of activity, as she was artistic and good at thinking up catchy rhyming slogans, but tonight her heart wasn't in it. Every now and then she'd look up from what she was doing and listen intently, sure she'd heard singing. But the night's sounds were nothing out of the ordinary: Martha playing her violin, Freya from the cabin two doors down, bawling, "Get in here, you daft mutt!" when her elderly spaniel wouldn't come inside after their evening walk, and the constant whistle of the wind through the bare branches of the beech trees.

When Zara laid a hand on her sleeve, she jumped.

"Are you feeling okay, Sage? You're really quiet tonight. Have you got another headache? I hope you're not coming down with something."

Kate, who was by the fire, stitching a bobble onto one of Zara's hats, looked up from her needle. "You don't need to come to the protest tomorrow afternoon if you don't fancy it. Maybe you need a wee rest."

"Yeah, I know that, guys. But I want to be there to see Duncan McPherson's face when he realises he's got a fight on his hands. Just struggling to come up with slogans. I'm a bit tired, I guess."

She finished writing

in bubble writing and handed the sign to Taj to colour with his felt pens. She'd written on stiff card instead of plywood, so it wouldn't do much harm even if Taj did decide to clobber Mr McPherson with it. Then she took a square piece of ply and painted her own slogan in dramatic red paint.

LEAVE
DUNLYRE HARBOUR
ALONE!

Big deal if it doesn't rhyme. Even if McPherson does build a marina here, we won't be around to see it. We'll be living elsewhere, campaigning for another cause.

She wished she still believed that she could change the world, the way Taj did. He was colouring with fierce determination, convinced his NO JET-SKIS HERE! sign would make a difference.

She forced a smile on her face. "That's amazing! The words really stand out now. Give it here and I'll tape it to this stick."

Zara smiled at her. "We've heard that McPherson and the television news team will be at the harbour at 2 p.m. We'll be there with our placards, making a noise. We might be on the telly!"

Trying not to cringe at this hideous prospect, Sage gave her mum a quick hug and went for her shower. When she thought about setting out first thing in the morning, her excitement began to hum like electricity.

And when she was brushing her teeth in front of the

mirror, she remembered seeing the face underwater; the not-quite-human, ghost-grey face, and she felt a tiny tremor of fear.

When Sage arrived at the castle at just after half eight, Finn was already there.

"Morning. You all set?" He grinned at her. "My dad, sister and evil stepmother are still in their beds. Lazy so-and-sos. I've left them a note, telling them I'm going for a run."

"I told my mums that I was going to my friend's house this morning to do some computer research about puffins, so if you've got any puffin facts up your sleeve, do let me know."

"Um, puffins nest in burrows. Their babies are called pufflings. 'Fraid that's the extent of my puffin awareness."

He stopped dead, and tugged Sage's sleeve. "Can you hear that? The merfolk are singing."

She couldn't reply, her brain tangled in a knot of unsettling emotions. But then a warm confidence began to radiate through her, and a spiky burst of energy. She grinned at Finn, trying to resist doing anything ridiculous, like high-fiving him or punching the air, and she could tell by his wide smile that he was feeling the same way.

But a grim-faced jogger who ran past, clutching a water bottle, didn't seem to notice anything unusual.

Finn pointed towards the beach. "We'd better get down there, while there's nobody around."

Side by side, they scrambled down the hillside that led to the beach. Sage had to cling to the long grass to stop her feet from slipping. A bitterly cold wind scoured her cheeks and tugged her hair into tangles. She wished she'd plaited it, because it would be a nightmare to comb. But at least the sun was out, weak and winter-pale, glimmering on the water.

"I'll deal with the kayak while you're getting changed," she said.

"No, wait for me. I'll help, once I'm ready." Finn unzipped his jacket and, like a conjuror with a string of flags, pulled out a large towel. "I brought a dry one in case yesterday's was still wet." He looked out to sea. "Do you think I'll be able to keep up with the kayak?"

"I'll go at your pace." Sage tugged off her boots. "We'll be able to stay fairly close to shore. Whin Bay isn't far."

She paused, as it dawned on her that she was being totally unlike her usual sensible, responsible self. "Are you okay after what happened yesterday? Are you sure you want to do this, Finn? I'll understand if you don't."

Finn's smile was super-confident. "Easy peasy."

One thing *was* easy: it was a breeze carrying the kayak across the rocks when there were two people involved.

"You should really be flying Flag Alpha," Finn said, as he

helped her push the kayak into the water. She gave him a quizzical look, and he explained. "It's a flag that's attached to the front of a boat to let other vessels know it's escorting a diver or a swimmer."

"If you'd told me about Flag Alpha last night I could have made one, while I was making my placard."

It was his turn to look puzzled, but she didn't say more. She was kicking herself for mentioning the placard. Finn was here on holiday; he wouldn't be interested in the whole saga of Duncan McPherson's plans to develop Dunlyre Harbour. And she wasn't about to tell him that her parents were leading the battle to stop the changes, or that she'd spent her entire childhood being dragged around from one campaign to the next. She'd much rather stick to talking about the merfolk.

Paddling at a slow, steady pace, Sage tried to remain within three metres of Finn as he did a strong front crawl through the water. They kept a short distance from shore, to avoid the rocks, but the waves weren't high. There was an icy wind, making the sails on passing yachts billow. The singing had stopped and the only sounds were the crying of the gulls and the distant chug of a fishing boat coming into the harbour.

For a while, Sage called words of encouragement and gave Finn the occasional thumbs up, until it dawned on her that he was probably unable to either see or hear her, as his goggles were misted and splattered with sea spray and his swim hat was pulled low over his head, covering his ears. The journey took much longer than if she'd been paddling alone, but eventually they rounded a large jagged rock and met the shallow curve of Whin Bay.

Sage leapt out and Finn helped her to pull the kayak up the beach over huge, lichen-speckled rocks.

She looked around. "Have to say, if there are any merfolk about, they're doing an impressive job of staying hidden."

"Or maybe we were right with the 'We're Both Going Crazy' theory." Finn tugged off his swim hat and goggles and grinned at her. "Right, let's explore the bay. No stone or shell unturned. We should split up. I'll go this way, you go the other. Course, most horror films start like this…"

"Bog off and find us some merfolk. And a flock of puffins would be handy while you're at it."

As Finn scrambled towards the tumbled rocks at the bottom of the cliff, Sage carried on along the shoreline. A huge stone tipped as she put weight on it, and she toppled, her bare foot splashing into a dank pool of kelp, her heel scraping against sharp rock.

Ow! Clumsy eejit.

She sat down and examined the large, bleeding graze on her foot.

I should've kept my boots on and risked them getting wet instead of leaving them back by the kayak cave.

And then, eerily, the singing started again, higher than the whistle of the wind. The song burbled and rippled like water, and Sage thought she could make out words, though it was hard to be sure. As she sat on the rock, she could feel the song's energy travelling through her body, coursing through her veins. The pain in her foot faded. When she looked down, the bleeding had stopped and the graze was healing, the damaged skin repairing itself as she stared, unblinking, hand over her mouth.

Oh, jeez. That's so freaking weird.

Lifting her foot and resting it on her thigh, she checked it closely. The injury had vanished, as if it had never been. Her skin tingled, and she felt lightheaded, euphoric.

The merfolk healed my foot! They're close. They're here.

As she clambered over the next heap of stones and jumped down, the singing stopped dead. Before Sage looked round, she waved frantically at Finn. "This way!"

And then, slowly, she turned her head.

13

SAGE

If it wasn't for the ripples in the rock pool made by their flicking tails, the two merchildren would have been almost impossible to spot. Their camouflage was incredibly effective, their grey-green skin merging seamlessly with the lichen blooming on the rocks. Their wet, straggly hair hung to their shoulders, the texture and colour of seaweed. As Sage drew nearer, she could see their pointed chins and wide eyes the colour of green sea-glass.

They're more like aliens than Ariel. The fairy stories and Disney movies are miles off. I wish Zara was here. She'd love to see real-life merfolk.

Shaking with nerves, she took another step forward. One of the merfolk hissed, and Sage felt her throat go dry. Fear trickled like ice water down her spine. When she'd listened to Zara's stories, she hadn't imagined the merfolk as scary, and she wished Finn

135

would hurry up and join her. Sage pulled the shell box from her jacket pocket. As she laid it on rocks at the edge of the merfolk's pool, the key caught on her sleeve and the box wobbled. Neither of the merfolk made a move to catch it.

Completely unnerved, Sage pointed at the cockle shell, still rocking gently back and forth. She couldn't prevent her voice from shaking. "This belongs to you. I found it on the beach at Dunlyre. You saved my friend Finn from drowning, and you gave him the key. We heard your singing. We found your map and we've come here because…"

Her voice trailed off, unable to explain why they'd come. The merfolk stayed silent, and it dawned on her that maybe Finn had imagined they'd spoken. Maybe they couldn't speak after all? So she pointed at the box again and mimed picking it up. She was flailing her arms around, pretending to be Finn, drowning, when she heard him clambering over the rocks behind her.

"What the heck are you doing?"

She heard him gasp but didn't look back, unable to tear her eyes from the merchildren, who remained statue-still, apart from their smooth, dolphin-grey tails, which flicked back and forth like pendulums.

Finn's voice was a strained croak. "They're a bit freaky-looking, aren't they?"

One of the merchildren hissed again and flicked his tail hard, splashing seawater over Finn's leg. Leaping backwards, Finn slipped on a patch of slimy kelp and landed on his backside.

Before she helped Finn to his feet, Sage saw the merchild's lips twitch into what might have been a smile. When he spoke again, Finn had the sense to whisper.

"Do they understand us?"

"I think so, yes. I think you just offended them." Sage tried to make amends with the merchildren, speaking louder: "Your singing is… incredible. You have very… um… distinctive voices."

"What do you want from us?" Finn blurted, clearly feeling Sage was being too slow to get to the point.

Again, a tail smacked against the pool's surface, causing a miniature tidal wave. Sage managed to leap out the way, but Finn got drenched.

He's going to catch a cold if he doesn't learn to be more tactful around merfolk.

For a long moment the merchildren sat silently, heads tilted. When they finally spoke, in unison, their voices fast as water bubbling over rocks, Sage and Finn had to edge closer to make out the words.

"We are Traigh and Muir, from the Undersea. Our songs are old, old… from the Land Time, before our Sea Time. We sang them when the great wave struck and washed away Cianalas." Both merchildren stretched out their hands, fingers webbed like a frog's. "Long ago, when Easgann Mòr followed us north, we sang our songs again."

Sage nodded. "And only the fisherman heard you, and he refused to help."

When Sage spoke, the merchildren turned their heads towards her and continued, in eerie unison. "Our elder, Mol, says humans are as useless as gold to selkies. But we thought if we sang to human children, a few might hear us, and might even have the courage to help. We sang, and you heard us. Only two, but hope filled our hearts. We took Mol's shell box and made the map so you could find us in a place we could talk without being seen. You heard us and you came. We are very glad to see you."

One of the merchildren emitted a series of strange clicking sounds.

"Land-speech, Traigh, or they will not understand." Muir turned back to Finn and Sage. "In our Land Time, we caught animals in traps, and fish in nets."

Sage blinked, her mind whirring.

Is she saying they were human children eight thousand years ago? And when they evolved into merfolk after the tsunami, they stayed as eternal children, never growing up? That is so weird.

"The merfolk have no use for such things, but we need them now." Traigh's Land-speech rushed like a river in

138

spate. "Have you got any with you today? Animal traps…
fishing nets?"

Finn tried to explain. "No, 'fraid not. Human kids
nowadays don't tend to use that stuff."

Muir's voice was a sad murmur. "Then you cannot help
us…"

Sage believed she understood.

*They must have heard about McPherson's plans and be
dreading the development.*

"You mustn't worry too much." She tried to speak in a
calm, soothing tone. "If the harbour development happens
at all, it'll be a long time before—"

Finn shook his head, took a step backwards. "There's
nothing can be done about the harbour development.
And, anyway, the thing is—"

Sage blinked in surprise, and was about to ask Finn how
he knew about the development, when Traigh broke in.

"Harbours are from the Land Time. We know little of
them, and care less." Traigh's voice was steeped in sadness.
"The merfolk can do nothing to prevent humans from
doing what they wish, and we have to live with it. They take
too many fish from the seas and the dolphins go hungry.
They dump rubbish so the seals must swim in dirty water.
We are asking for your help with a threat to our lives, to all
the merfolk's lives, if you would only listen!"

Sage stepped forward to lay a reassuring hand on

Traigh's shoulder, then wished she hadn't. His skin felt cold and clammy. "We're listening. Aren't we, Finn? And we'll do our best to help."

Finn nodded, but she could see doubt in his eyes. "Yeah, we'll do our best, though obvs there's nothing we can do to help with underwater stuff."

Liquid pooled in Muir's sea-green eyes. "It is too much to ask. I understand that now. You will not be able to fight Easgann Mòr."

A shudder of fear ran right through Sage. "Easgann Mòr? The sea monster? I thought she lived up north, in the sea lochs."

"She is here in the firth. Traigh saw her, at the last neap tide, although he has not seen her since." Muir's voice was swamped in grief. "We are the last of our kind. If Easgann Mòr kills us, merfolk are gone forever. But the other merfolk do not believe us, as Traigh has often thought he has glimpsed the monster before and been mistaken. Yet this is different. We have tried to tell them that we must leave right away or she will find us, and then the carnage will be terrible, as it was in the north, when we lost so many."

Traigh began to shiver, clearly traumatised by a thousand-year-old memory. Muir gazed at Sage and spoke to her as if the others weren't there. "My brother has been deeply affected by these terrible memories, but this time the Great Eel's head rose right out of the water in front of him.

There is no doubt." Her tone sharpened. "And Traigh is not a liar or a troublemaker, whatever Mol might think."

"I believe him." Finn's eyes were anxious. "Yesterday… yesterday I was out in a boat with my dad, and I thought I saw something huge moving in the water. You need to persuade the others to leave."

Sage gasped, horrified. "You never told me *that*!"

"Well, I would have, if I'd known someone else had seen it too! I thought I was imagining things."

Sage opened her mouth and closed it again. She was floundering. The merfolk's problem was a much bigger, more frightening and more immediate danger than she'd expected. It seemed to be too large, literally, for two kids to tackle on their own.

I don't think we'll be able to save them. I don't think there's anything we can do…

"You must have nets at least!" There was desperation in Traigh's voice. "You can bring them to us and we can trap the eel, as the fisherman did—"

"Silence, Traigh!" Muir cut in. "Our secrets are not for human ears."

She gave a huge, bubbling sigh. "We are doomed. It is too big a problem for you to solve."

"We're so sorry." Sage felt salt tears stinging her eyes. "Can't you have another go at trying to persuade the other merfolk?"

141

"They will not believe us." Muir's shoulders slumped. "Besides, they do not want to leave the firth because so many creatures here need our help."

Finn glanced up and down the beach. "Really? There doesn't seem to be that much wildlife around, apart from the odd seagull."

Silence fell, and Sage wondered if Finn was going to get another soaking. But then Muir and Traigh spoke in unison. "Even though you cannot help us, we really are grateful to you for coming. Before you leave, follow us, and we will show you something."

Together, the merchildren slid off the rocks, moving so fast that Sage jumped back, startled. They rippled across the stony beach, their bodies undulating like seals'.

Sage and Finn followed along the shoreline until the merchildren dragged themselves up a large boulder with their impressively strong forearms. Muir put a webbed hand to her lips. "We never disturb them unless they need our help."

Warily, Sage clambered up the boulder and peeped over it. Finn hauled himself up beside her and was the first to spot them.

"Wow. Look!" he whispered.

But she'd seen them now too. "Oh, look at that one! It's laughing!"

On this narrow stretch of shore, a small freshwater

stream gushed down the cliff face, over the rocks and into the sea. Sliding down this natural waterslide was an otter cub, its fur sleek and glistening wet, joy on its furry face. It reached the shore and began wrestling with its sibling in the sand, rolling and play-biting, while a third cub scratched its fur against the rocks, then splashed into the sea and twirled in the waves beside its mother.

Finn pointed at the cub in the water. "That wee otter could do with a wetsuit. It's freezing in there."

"They have two layers of fur." Traigh's voice bubbled with pride, as if they were treasured pets. "A thick undercoat that traps air and a waterproof topcoat. They float better than you do."

"Oh, ha ha. Very funny."

Sage turned to Muir and grinned. "Aw, aren't they sweet!"

Muir's mouth curved into an almost-there smile. "Adorable, but their teeth are sharp! We take care of them when they are injured and tend them when they are sick." Then her smile vanished. "When we merfolk realised we could live forever, we wondered what we should do with our time. We chose to live our lives caring for the creatures of the shore and the sea."

"That's lovely. It really is…" Sage bit her lip. "But did you get a say in that decision?"

Muir's tiny smile vanished. She shook her head,

spraying seawater. "No. Mol and the other adults make all the decisions. Traigh and I are never consulted."

And they clearly don't get to enjoy themselves… ever.

Sage watched as two of the cubs scrambled a little way up the cliff face and came skidding down the stream, sliding on their tummies over the smooth, wet rock. She loved the happy expressions on their faces.

"That looks like fun," she said thoughtfully. "Do you think the otters would mind if we joined in their games, just this once?"

The merchildren stared at her, and for a moment she thought she'd angered them. Then, both merchildren slid off the boulder into the water and swam round to where the shore met the stream.

"Come!" called Muir. "They will not be afraid if you are with us."

Finn's eyes brightened. "Coming?" he asked Sage.

She nodded and slid off the rock.

As the sun rose higher and the tide crept in, Finn and the merchildren took turns hurtling down the natural water slide, while Sage played chase with the otter cubs, splashing in and out of the shallow water, keeping her bare feet well clear of their tiny, needle-sharp teeth. Muir seemed to be enjoying herself, rolling with the otters across the rocks and splashing into the water, flicking her tail in a rock pool. Sage kicked her legs, and the otters spun in the frothing water, loving their whirlpool bath.

"Watch this for a landing!" yelled Finn, launching himself from a rock and shooting headfirst down the slippery slope.

Sage grimaced as he belly-flopped into the sea and sank like a stone. As he resurfaced, one of the otters followed him down the slope and slid smoothly into the water, a smug smile on its face.

Sage burst out laughing.

"Face it, Finn. The otters are miles better than you at both staying afloat *and* diving!"

Out at sea, a ship's horn blasted. The otters looked up, alarmed, and all four scurried off into the long grass on the cliff face, heading back to the safety of their holt.

"Aw, shame. That was incredible." Finn sounded awestruck. "I've never even seen otters in the wild before, never mind had the chance to go on a freaking water slide with them."

Muir rolled off the rocks in one smooth movement and splashed into the sea.

"This bay has been a safe haven for the otter family. But we will not be here to protect them for much longer."

Sadness swept over Sage. For a little while she'd forgotten the terrible danger the merfolk were in. She and Finn might never see them again.

"It was… incredible to meet you both. Thank you for

showing us the otters. They were amazing too." She spoke in the upbeat tone she used to cheer up Taj on school days. "We'll think of something, won't we Finn? We'll come back and see you soon, when we've thought of a plan."

Finn cleared his throat. "Sage, we need to go."

He was right, they did need to go, but Sage felt horribly guilty to be leaving. And she was afraid for herself and Finn too. They had to get back in the water now, aware of the danger lurking there, and Finn didn't even have the protection of a kayak.

"We'll stick really close to shore," she told him, trying to maintain a positive, reassuring tone. "So if we spot anything… anything worrying… we can get back on land super-quickly."

As she paddled back to Dunlyre, the merchildren began to sing, a desolate, grief-stricken song that wrenched at her heart. Tears poured down Sage's cheeks. She wondered if Finn, swimming beside the kayak, could hear the song, and if he felt the same guilt, or was just desperate to get out of the sea. Fear gripped her as she realised she might have to come back here alone.

It was after eleven, but the sun was too weak to take the chill from the air as they climbed back up the hill towards the castle. Despite being encased in boots and cosy socks, Sage's feet felt bone-cold after being exposed for so long, and Finn looked worn out after his long swim. When they reached the top, he stood, shuffling his feet, refusing to look at her, swinging his overstuffed rucksack. She wondered how he'd explain the damp wetsuit and two sodden towels.

"Well, it's been a thrill-ride, but I really need to get home. My dad will be wondering what's keeping me."

A horrible sinking sensation settled in the pit of Sage's stomach.

He thinks it's over. He's saying goodbye.

She stayed silent, hoping he'd prove her wrong. But he still wouldn't look her in the eye. Instead, he was staring out to sea, his mouth set in a tight line. "We can't help them, Sage. You do realise that, don't you? We can't go back. Do you know how scared I was swimming back here, knowing a massive monster might be below me, slithering around in the water? Have you seen the jaws on a moray eel? Or the teeth on a conger? Even regular-sized eels are freaky. A monster one is the stuff of nightmares."

He wasn't wrong. Eels gave her the creeps, with their staring eyes and long, sinuous, snake-like bodies. But...

"And even if we were brave or daft enough to get in the water with a monster," Finn continued. "What would we do to stop her, exactly? How could we prevent Easgann Mòr from attacking the merfolk? Or us? Slap her with my swim hat?"

147

"We'll think of something." Her voice rose as desperation set in. "We can't just leave them to get killed!"

"What about us? Even the merfolk don't believe the eel is here, apart from Traigh and Muir, so it would be us against Easgann Mòr. And if she's as big as the Loch Ness Monster, then we're… we're out of our depth."

She didn't want to hear. "Well, I'm going to try. On my own if I have to. The merfolk have healing powers. They fixed my sore foot. And that must be why you got better so fast yesterday. Even if we get hurt by the eel, I'm sure they'd be able to heal us."

"You think? Sage, Muir and Traigh are immortal, and they're still scared. I reckon when someone has been chewed up and spat out by a sea monster they'll be beyond fixing."

When he turned to face her, his shoulders were slumped, his expression resigned. "Look, I really need to go. My dad will be… I'll see you around."

She watched him head off, her lips pressed tight to stop herself from crying. It had been such an adventure, searching for the merfolk, and it had been so exciting to find them. But Finn was right, it was hopeless. The merchildren's problem was too big. They couldn't help. Still, it infuriated her that he wouldn't even try, and she was gutted that she'd lost a friend.

When Finn was no longer in sight, she stood by

the castle letting waves of sadness wash over her. Her fingers felt for the shell's comforting warmth, until she remembered she'd given it back.

The magic had gone.

When she looked out to sea, though, light was flickering on the waves, and the firth shone like burnished gold. In the distance, the Grey Isle's granite rocks glittered silver. Touched by sunshine, the world seemed to glisten. Anything was possible.

"I haven't got a plan yet," she whispered. "But I'll think of something."

14

FINN

As he headed uphill, Finn looked out to the sea, half hoping to catch a glimpse of the merfolk. There had been such desperation in the merchildren's voices, and their singing had wrenched at his heart as he'd swum away. He wished he could save them.

But there's nothing we can do to help them. Surely Sage can see that?

The first thing he heard when he opened the front door was Lizzy's voice. She didn't sound happy. Rolling his eyes, Finn closed the door quietly behind him, pulled his damp wetsuit out of the rucksack and hung it inside the zip-up wet-bag hanging from a peg in the porch.

Sorted. If I don't bring this in, and if I drop the towels on the bathroom floor, nobody will be any the wiser.

As he was about to open the other door, Dad spoke, his voice tight and defensive. Finn listened, curious to know what he and Lizzy were arguing about.

"I know he's upset with me!" A newspaper rustled, and Finn could picture his dad's irritated face, annoyed at having to abandon the paper and focus on matters closer to home. "And yes, I should have told him I had work to do while we're here, I know that, but I was scared he wouldn't come at all. You know what he's been like recently."

Finn heard his gran's voice muttering in his ear.

I telt you, lad. Eavesdroppers never hear any guid o' themselves.

He didn't particularly want to hear what he'd been like recently, and was about to open the porch door and make his presence known. But Lizzy was speaking now, her voice more upset than he'd ever heard, and his hand stilled on the handle.

"You need to try and put yourself in his shoes, Tom. I know what it feels like when your parents split up. It's horrible." She gave a heavy sigh. "At least you and Helen manage to be civil to one another. My mum and dad still haven't got a nice word to say about each other after nearly twenty years living apart. I can't mention one parent without the other pulling a face, and they never think about how that makes their kids feel. They're a complete nightmare, like I said to my sister on the phone that day, when Mum refused to come to our house-warming if Dad was going to be there. I can't believe poor Finn thought I was talking about him and Ava."

There was a short silence, and Finn froze, scared she'd heard his sharp intake of breath.

"You're lucky to have such great kids, Tom, and you need to put them first. Stay on good terms with your ex-wife and stop prioritising your job over time spent with your kids, you big lummox."

He heard his father sigh, could imagine him running his hands through his hair, as he always did when he was feeling harassed. Yet Finn wasn't focusing on his dad, but on what Lizzy had just said.

She wasn't talking about Ava and me on the phone that day.

All this time, her words had been echoing in his head, hurting his heart: "Honestly, Claire, the two of them are a complete nightmare…" She'd meant her parents! He'd thought Lizzy was a two-faced cow, only being nice to their faces. It felt weird to realise he'd got it so wrong.

Finn heard his dad's footsteps heading across the room. His first reaction was to shrink back against the coats and jackets, but almost instantly he realised that was crazy.

If he finds me in here, they'll know I've been listening. Get in there, quick.

When he pushed open the inner door, Lizzy's smile was warm and he could see the relief in her eyes. "Oh, we were getting worried about you!"

"Where have you been?" snapped Dad, waving the note he'd left. "A bloomin' run? You've been away for ages!

You really need to get back when you say you will."

"Sorry… I went for a *really* long run along the cliffs. It was a lovely bright morning. I'm starving. Does anyone want toast? Where's Ava?"

"She's in the back garden, creating a nest for the robins." Lizzy pointed out the window at Ava, who was halfway up a tree in her Cinderella costume and wellies, stuffing twigs and soggy moss into a crevice in the trunk. She smiled at Finn a little uncertainly. "And I'd like some toast, if you're making it."

"Sure. Marmalade or jam?"

"Um, jam, thanks."

He just knew Dad and Lizzy were looking at each other, mouthing, *What's got into him?* behind his back, but he didn't really care.

"If you're both hungry, why don't we go back to the cafe for brunch instead?" Dad was already putting on his coat. "It was nice yesterday, wasn't it?"

This time Finn had fish and chips, which was a weird first meal of the day, but very tasty. Ava kept up a constant stream of excited chatter. Finn, deep in thought, let her voice wash over him.

Right, so a sea monster is in the Firth of Clyde. She's hunting for merfolk to kill and eat. But what can I do about it? What can anybody do about it? Blow her up? Harpoon her?

Ideas were whirling in his brain when he realised Dad was talking to Lizzy about the harbour development.

"I'll be glad when this commission is over. It's been months of wrangling with the professional do-gooders, but the final planning meeting is tomorrow and hopefully it'll go our way."

Lizzy's expression clouded. "They're environmentalists, Tom, not professional do-gooders! I work for a charity, so I guess that's me too?"

His dad flushed. "No, don't be daft. They're claiming otters have been seen in the area, but who knows? Anyway, if the otters don't fancy the construction work I'm sure they'll swim off somewhere else."

Lizzy didn't look convinced. "Otters are a protected species, you know. Are you sure this is what Dunlyre needs?"

"Lizzy, people in this area are crying out for jobs. Anyway, I'm not the boss in this situation. What my client wants, my client gets, or my head'll be on a platter."

Finn couldn't stop himself. "I saw some otters this morning. When I was out for my… run, I saw a family of otters, playing on the rocks. A mother and three cubs."

Lizzy and Dad looked genuinely impressed. "Wow! You lucky thing!" Lizzy gasped. "I've never seen otters in the wild. You'll need to take us all to see them tomorrow."

It dawned on Finn that he'd just put his foot right in it.

Stupid eejit. We can't access Whin Bay on foot. If Dad checks, he'll realise I've been swimming. And anyway, even if I admit I swam there, we can't go again. The water is too dangerous.

"Um, that might be a bad idea. The otters might be scared away by so many people. I mean, I think they're quite shy."

"Yeah, you may be right." Dad's voice was flat, his gaze disappointed. "Perhaps we should leave them in peace, eh?"

He thinks I don't want to show Lizzy the otters. He thinks I'm being a git.

His father paid the bill, then held the door open so they could file out of the cafe. Finn shuffled out, still cringing. He was about to try and explain further when Ava shrieked, "Look, Daddy! There's Mr Ferson! Lots of people are chasing him!"

She wasn't wrong. A group of about a dozen people waving placards were following Duncan McPherson and a local TV crew down the path from the car park. They were chanting, and as they drew nearer, Finn could make out the words.

"No marina in Dunlyre!"

"No jet-skis!"

"Keep our coastline peaceful!"

"Save the otters!"

Lizzy grabbed Ava's hand. "Come on, sweetheart. We'll pop into the craft shop around the corner and see if we can buy something nice for Daddy and Finn's Christmas."

She whisked Ava away just as Duncan McPherson reached the bottom of the hill, red-faced and scowling.

"I might have known this lot would turn up." He beckoned to the camera crew. "Guys, this is Tom Robertson, my architect."

Finn's eyes were on the protestors heading towards them, when he recognised one, and froze.

Is that Sage?

Even from a distance he could see the flicker of horror in her eyes as she recognised him too. And no wonder she looked upset, when he was standing right beside the enemy.

"Leave Dunlyre Harbour alone!" she yelled, waving her placard as she marched towards them, cheeks flushed, eyes flashing, her long dark hair whipped by the wind.

McPherson gave an exasperated sigh. "Hopefully they'll leave shortly and you guys will be able to interview me in peace."

He turned, just as Sage thrust her placard towards him.

"Oi, you be careful, young lady! You nearly hit me!"

Sage turned towards the TV camera. "Is that thing on?" When the cameraman nodded, she started to speak, her voice ringing out across the harbour. "This marina will be a disaster! We have otters here, cormorants, oystercatchers and seals. Mr McPherson is planning to hire out jet-skis and speedboats. Imagine the terrible damage fast boats could do to a poor wee seal pup, or to an otter cub out for its first swim. Think of Dunlyre's birds being poisoned by petrol fumes, or being so terrified by the noise that they leave here and never come back!" Her voice cracked, and she looked as if she was about to cry. "Dunlyre is the wrong place for this marina, and I really hope the planning committee can see that and tell Duncan McPherson to go home and think again."

McPherson laughed. "I think this one imagines she's in a movie, playing the pesky kid who's trying to thwart the baddies! She's clearly been watching too much telly."

"I don't have a TV at home, so that's mince," Sage continued, her expression as fierce as her tone. "We've been telling you for ages, Mr McPherson. You and the planning committee need to do what's right for Dunlyre." She turned, and her eyes bored into Finn's. "You need to do the right thing."

He stood, blinking like an owl, as the camera swivelled towards his father. The interviewer held up his microphone.

"So, Mr Robertson, what do you have to say to the people who believe your proposals are a disaster for the local environment?"

Mortified, Finn slipped away.

Up by the castle there was a bench looking over the cliff edge and out to sea, and he slumped onto it, ignoring the damp that seeped through his jeans. He'd only been sitting for a couple of minutes, watching a small sailing boat battling the wind, when Sage appeared and plonked herself down at his side. They sat in silence for a moment, and then she spoke, her voice stiff.

"Hey. You didn't say you were on the Dark Side."

Annoyance bubbled like acid. What right did she have to judge him? "You didn't ask, but now you mention it, I'm not on McPherson's side. I don't like him." He stood up. "But my dad's an architect. It's not a crime."

She sprang to her feet, eyes burning with anger. "It would be a crime to have jet-skis here... You must see that!"

Finn put his head in his hands.

If I was going to be really honest, I'd tell her I had brilliant fun the last time Dad and I went jet-ski-ing, but I'd also like the merfolk and the otters to be left in peace, so if the decision was up to me, I'd feel a bit torn, and I'm glad it's up to the planners.

"Don't you care, Finn? Don't you want to make a difference?"

He looked up. "We're kids. The development's not our problem."

Sage rolled her eyes at him.

He turned away, his words echoing eerily in his head.

Not our problem...

He'd said that before. And as he stared out towards the sun-splashed sea, he remembered when and where.

Gran had taken him on the train to Irvine, just the two of them. It had been a glorious, sun-kissed afternoon, and they'd had ice-creams with chocolate Flakes from the cafe at the harbour and then walked along the long beach. Some picnickers had been there before them and left their rubbish behind, littering the sand. To Finn's embarrassment, Gran had pulled a carrier bag from her pocket and started picking up discarded crisp packets and Coke cans as they walked along.

"Just leave it, Gran," he'd hissed. "It's not our rubbish. It's not our problem."

Her steely glare had made him wince. "Oh, aye it is our ruddy problem! We're not like those manky litter louts. We care, and we're going tae leave this beach better than we found it." Then her eyes had softened, and she'd smiled at him. "So, off you go and fetch that Irn Bru bottle, an' I'll pick up yon sweetie wrapper."

Traigh and Muir are *my problem... They asked me for help. And I care. I don't want the merfolk to get killed...*

When he spoke, there was a slight, but annoying, waver in his voice. "You were great, Sage. The way you stood up to McPherson was amazing. But now, can we forget the blooming harbour development? We can do zilch about it. Leave that stuff to the adults."

"Forget the harbour development?" Sage growled. "It's *the* issue for my parents, and the only reason we're living here."

He spoke before he'd had time to think. "So you're living in Dunlyre just so your parents can fight the harbour development? They've put this fight before what's best for you and your brother?"

Sage stared at him, shocked. "Taj and I are fine, thanks very much!" She fell silent for a moment. "Actually, we really are fine. Kate and Zara are great parents. They care about the environment and they've taught us to care too. We've lived in lots of amazing places. Life isn't perfect, but it's absolutely fine." A smile twitched at the corners of her mouth. "Though you do realise I'm fraternising with the enemy?"

"Well, you'll need to keep doing it if we're going to work together to save the merfolk."

"So, you're going to help? You've decided? We're going to save the merfolk?"

When he nodded, her smile got even wider.

"Okay, let's do it."

And then his phone buzzed. Irritated by the interruption, he read the message and then shoved the phone back in his pocket.

"I need to go." He paused. "Why don't we meet early tomorrow, just after dawn? I've got a plan, and if you think it makes sense, we can go back to Whin Bay and tell the merchildren. It's too late to do anything now anyway. It'll be dark soon."

"Tell me now, cos if it's rubbish I'll need time to come up with something better."

"No time to explain. But feel free to come up with Plans B to Z."

"In case your plan is mince, you mean?"

He nodded, and grinned at Sage, trying to ignore the thought of what else tomorrow might bring. But as he turned to walk away, it swept over him, unstoppable as a breaking wave.

When we go back to Whin Bay, Sage will be in a tiny kayak and I'll be swimming. And there's a monster in that water. She might be after the merfolk, but Sage and I will be in terrible danger too.

15

SAGE

At home, Kate and Zara enveloped Sage in hugs, both almost bursting with pride.

"You were incredible!" Kate's cheeks were flushed with pleasure. "That architect fellow didn't know what to say to follow your speech. He just mumbled something non-committal about the application being in the hands of the planning committee. McPherson looked fit to explode."

Sage was hardly listening. All evening, all she could think of was the merfolk and the monster.

In the middle of the night, she was jerked awake by a cry in the darkness, and it took her a moment to realise it wasn't a merchild's high-pitched shriek.

"Taj? What's wrong?"

Taj could hardly speak between hiccupping sobs. "I had a bad dream. About the bad boy."

A chill ran through Sage. Sliding down from the top bunk, she squeezed in beside him. When she hugged him, his face against hers was wet with tears. And probably snot from his runny nose, though she tried not to think about that.

"What are you talking about, Taj? What bad boy?"

"A big boy in Primary 5. I think his name is Ewan. He calls me Fart Boy and he keeps nipping my arm and pushing me against the wall. I don't like it, Sage. I don't ever want to go back to school."

Guilt twisted in Sage's stomach.

I knew all along there was something wrong. I've just been too wrapped up in myself to pay him any attention.

"Oh, Taj. Has this been going on for a long time? Why didn't you tell me?"

"I told you nobody likes me."

"Yes, you did. But you didn't tell me you were being bullied." She sighed. "We'll talk to Zara and Kate. As soon as school starts back, they'll tell the headteacher, and Ewan-Stinky-Fart-Boy will be in deep trouble."

Even in the darkness, she knew her brother was grinning.

"And also, you can point Ewan-Smelly-Poop-Features out to me in the playground and I'll have a wee chat with him."

Taj's voice was awestruck. "Will you punch him in the face?"

"No, Taj, don't be daft. Violence isn't the answer. There are better ways to deal with bullies. Go to sleep. Everything's going to be okay."

She fell asleep, and woke stiff and uncomfortable, hanging off the edge of the bottom bunk. It was only as she was creeping out of the front door, swathed in a scarf to protect her face from the early morning's chill, that her words echoed in her head.

There are better ways to deal with bullies.

But what was the best way to handle one the size and ferocity of Easgann Mòr?

By the time she arrived at the beach, darkness was being leached from the sky by the rising sun, its rays reflected as ripples of gold in a pewter sea.

Finn had already changed into his wetsuit and had a huge fluffy towel wrapped round him like a shawl. He looked tired and nervous, but he grinned at her and gave her a thumbs up.

"What does it feel like to be famous?"

"Huh?"

"Your blasting of Duncan McPherson was on last night's local news."

She grimaced, torn between being proud and horrified. "That's something, at least. It's the final planning meeting today."

"Yeah, I know. My dad's going," Finn replied.

Sage had left a note for her parents, wishing them good luck at their protest outside the council offices but saying she was sorry she couldn't come along, as she was meeting her friend this morning so their project would be complete before Christmas.

While they half carried, half pushed the kayak across the beach, Finn outlined his plan. It was certainly simple, but Sage doubted it would be effective.

"So, basically, we ask Traigh and Muir to take us to their island home, persuade the merfolk they're in danger, and ask them to stay out of the water until the monster gives up and goes away?"

"Yeah, that's about it. It's the best I could do at short notice. Do you have a better idea?"

Sage sighed and shook her head. "Nope. But there are a few flaws in your plan. First, only Muir believes Traigh. The rest of them think he's the Merkid Who Cried Wolf. Second, why didn't the merfolk just do that the last time Easgann Mòr attacked? There has to be a reason. Third—"

Finn waved his towel in surrender and then placed it in the kayak's front hatch.

"Okay, I get it." His voice was flat, and she wondered if he was upset she wasn't more enthusiastic about his plan. "I was freezing yesterday," he muttered, attempting to stuff his jacket into the kayak's hatch.

She bit her lip, vaguely annoyed that he hadn't asked permission. *It's my kayak...*

"Maybe if you hadn't kept offending the merfolk, you'd not have got splashed so often."

"Good point. I did keep putting my size nines in it."

She gave him a hand to cram the jacket inside, but warned, "If the kayak rolls, and it's done that loads of times before, everything will get soaked."

"I'll risk it."

Finn took time to get acclimatised to the water temperature, while she practised her sweep stroke, turning the kayak in slow circles. After a few minutes they set off, heading towards Whin Bay.

At first Sage was nervous, and her eyes darted, wondering if that dark ripple was growing into a long shadow in the deep, or if that soft scrape against the hull wasn't an underwater rock after all. But her confidence grew as she got into the flow, paddling strongly with smooth forward strokes, all her muscles feeling the strain, enjoying the feeling of gliding through the water.

The sea breeze was icy cold, but the winter sun was above the horizon, a glowing orange disc in a psychedelic sky. It was a beautiful morning and she felt glad to be here, just as much part of the scene as the gulls soaring above her. Close behind her, Finn was swimming a confident freestyle.

He's being really brave, but I bet he's— Hey, what the heck was that?

A jolt jerked her forward, as if the kayak had hit something hard. She glanced over the side, nerves jangling.

What if Easgann Mòr's down there, preparing to strike? At least I'm in the boat. Finn will have no chance. He didn't really want to come. It'll be my fault if he gets killed.

When she looked behind, the blood in her veins ran cold. Finn was no longer swimming in her wake. He was nearby but heading in the wrong direction. It was as if he was being dragged out to sea.

"Finn!" Horror constricted her throat and the word came out as a choked gasp. She heard a shout, shredded by the wind.

And then the kayak began to turn. At first Sage fought, doing frantic sweep strokes in the opposite direction, but it was hopeless. The boat seemed to be moving of its own accord, cutting through the sea like an arrow zipping towards its target. Giving up the battle, Sage lifted the paddle out of the water and, dreading what she might see, leaned to the right. At first she could only make out a dark, indistinct shape, and a shudder ran through her, but as her eyes adjusted to the dimness she saw that there was more than one creature below the boat. Two broad-shouldered merfolk were pushing the kayak along, using their tail flukes to produce a thrust that shot their bodies through

167

the water at incredible speed. Ahead, a tail flapped against the sea's surface, splattering water.

They're too large to be Traigh and Muir. It's the adults! And they've got Finn too.

Her heart thudded and her fingers tightened on the paddle's shaft.

How do they know about us? What's happened?

A leaden grey rock loomed ahead and it dawned on her where they were going. She and Finn had been right from the beginning. The Grey Isle wasn't an uninhabited island after all.

It was the home of the merfolk.

Sage braced herself for impact as the kayak shot across the shingle and came to a stop, wedged between two rocks. Struggling out of the buoyancy aid, she popped it inside the hatch and pulled out Finn's towel. She was determined to focus on the essentials before facing everything else. Finn had been dumped unceremoniously on a ledge, but his face was shining with excitement.

"Did you see that? Did you check the speed these guys can move?" He peeled off his swim hat, gave himself a quick dry, and pulled on his jacket. The tide was out, exposing a small shingle beach and a wide expanse of limpet-encrusted rocks. It was freezing cold on the exposed islet, and they both put up their hoods. Finn was still buzzing with adrenalin, firing off questions she couldn't answer.

"Where are they? Where did they go? Are they still in the water?"

Sage looked around, searching for any sign of the merfolk, then blinked and stared, her heart racing. Overwhelmed, she took a step back, towards the safety of the kayak, and stepped on Finn's foot.

"Ow!"

"Sorry, but…"

She grabbed his sleeve, leaned in and whispered in his ear.

"They're here, Finn. All around us. Look closer."

Almost invisible, the merfolk sat, staring, the greyish skin on their upper bodies merging with the lichen-stained rocks, their tails dipped in pools of brackish water. Some scraped at limpets, others dried their wet hair, squeezing dripping strands between their webbed fingers. One, with semi-translucent green hair and a tail criss-crossed with deep scars, was perched on a high rock, staring out to the sea.

Finn's voice was a frog's croak. "Okay, I'm freaked out now. Same?"

"Same… Finn, what were we thinking?"

"No freaking clue."

Close to the water's edge, Traigh, Muir and a smaller merchild watched, their eyes round and anxious. The silence was eerie, but then the smallest merchild whistled.

"Hush, Cuan. Humans cannot speak Undersea," whispered Muir, and then winced when a voice boomed.

"Silence!"

Slowly, the merman on the high rock turned to face the new arrivals. "I am Mol, elder of the merfolk of Cianalas."

Sage swallowed nervously. There was something very intimidating about the elder's chilly, ocean-blue eyes.

"Last night, I caught Muir returning my treasure to its hiding place." Mol held up a cockle shell, which Sage recognised immediately. "Traigh and Muir have confessed to the theft, and to instigating contact with humans. They were very foolish to involve humans in Undersea business, especially when there is no evidence we are in any danger. We have brought you children here... to bring this matter to an end."

Sage felt her knees weaken. Beside her, Finn swallowed hard.

Traigh's tail slapped hard against a rock. "You are the one who is wrong, Mol! Easgann Mòr is in the firth. The human boy has seen her too."

There was a pause, then Mol's eyes fixed on Finn. "Is this true?"

"I think so. I mean, I can't be a hundred per cent sure. The waves were high. My dad thought it could be seals, but I—"

"You see, Traigh? He is not sure. It could have been seals." Mol's voice crashed like waves. "And you, Traigh?

How many times have you claimed to see Easgann Mòr and been wrong? Nine, ten? More?"

The merchild's head drooped, and Sage felt anger grow in her chest.

That's not fair. It isn't Traigh's fault. If I'd survived a massacre — twice — I'd be super-anxious too.

"We've got a plan." She hugged herself, unable to stop trembling. "We've come to help you."

"We have no need of human help!" When Mol roared, revealing sharp incisors, Sage's mouth went sandpaper dry. "Tell them, Eilean. My anger is too great."

Eilean's dark hair was the rough texture of bladderwrack seaweed, but her voice was calm and soothing, words trickling like water over pebbles.

"As you wish. Greetings, children. I am Eilean, an elder of the merfolk council. When we saw you heading for Whin Bay, we decided it would be best if you came here instead. We need to ask you a favour, and we hope you will grant it."

Sage saw relief in Finn's eyes. Mol's talk of bringing the matter to an end had clearly made him nervous too.

She nodded at Eilean. "Sure. What do you want us to do?"

"All we need you to do is forget us. Keep our existence a secret from the rest of humankind. That is all. Tell nobody."

Sadness swirled in Sage's stomach, but she nodded again. "I won't say a word. Not to a living soul."

"Me neither." Finn sounded unhappy too. "But I think—"

Mol broke in. "We are quite safe, I assure you. Please do as Eilean asks: leave now and tell no one you have seen us."

The leader waved a webbed hand in Traigh and Muir's direction.

"We have made another decision this morning. You two are to be forgiven, this time, but any more trouble and you will be banished. Now, you will assist these two children back to shore and you will *never* try to contact humans again. Learn from your mistake, as I did, long ago, with the fisherman. Go now. All of you."

Traigh and Muir looked utterly defeated, shoulders slumped, faces half hidden behind their kelp-like hair. As Sage dragged the kayak off the beach, a tear ran down her chilled face.

Traigh saw the monster's head rise out of the water! He couldn't be mistaken about that. I can't believe that we're being made to leave now, while the merfolk are still in terrible danger. But what else can we do?

Finn was standing right at the water's edge when he turned back to face Mol. "What if Traigh's right and Easgann Mòr is in the firth? Until you're sure it's safe, you should stay on the Grey Isle. Don't go in the water…"

172

His voice trailed away. Sage glanced up, and blinked.

Only Traigh, Muir and little Cuan were still visible. The bodies of the adult merfolk seemed to have merged with the rocks, and with their eyes closed, they were almost completely hidden in their grey-green camouflage.

No wonder humans think merfolk are mythical. When they want to be, they're virtually invisible.

"Staying out of the sea is not possible." Muir moved across the beach, her body crunching on the shingle. "At night we sleep with our tails in the water, or our skin dries out and cracks. In daytime we can stay on dry land for an hour or two at most. We have to keep swimming, even when danger threatens."

Traigh's voice was drenched in sadness. "A grim choice: die from dehydration or be eaten alive. Come, we will take you back to shore. It is over."

16

FINN

As Finn slid off a rock into waist-deep water, the smallest merchild dived in beside him and splashed around, playful as an otter cub, somersaulting and twisting until the water was whisked into foam.

"You are wet enough now. Go back to the land, Cuan," ordered Traigh.

Cuan's lips pursed. "Mol says we are safe in the Undersea."

"You can help me push, Cuan." With a quiet splash, Muir rolled into the sea, emerging behind the kayak. "Traigh, you guide the boy, in case he goes under again."

Stung, Finn felt the urge to protest. "My name's Finn. Also, I've no plans to drown."

Cuan giggled. "Fish have fins. If you are a fish, why can you not swim in the Undersea?"

Finn splashed him.

Swimming beside the merchildren was an exhilarating, exhausting experience. Cuan was bubbling with excitement and kept abandoning the kayak to come and swim beside Finn. Traigh's butterfly stroke was incredible, and although Finn tried to match it, stroke by stroke, he found it impossible. He'd have to train eight hours a day to build anything like as much strength and stamina. Even when he swam with as much power as he possessed, he struggled to equal little Cuan's speed.

Finn's swim hat covered his ears, but even so, when they were about halfway to Dunlyre, he heard the piercing, warning shrieks of the herring gulls overhead. The merchildren broke their silence, emitting a cacophony of rapid clicks and high-pitched whistles. Finn stopped and began treading water so he could see what was going on.

In the distance, close to the Grey Isle, the herring gulls screamed, swooping low, their wings beating off the water. When Finn shaded his eyes, he could make out huge slate-grey humps, the girth of a boat's funnel, rising up out of the waves.

Fear made Finn's heartbeat race. He'd seen that heaving, sinuous form once before – from the Wayfarer.

"Jeez, what the heck's that?" Sage called. "Is it a whale? It's a freaking monst…"

Her voice died away as she realised.

The merchildren had spotted the monster too.

Cuan's voice was a shrill shriek. "Easgann Mòr!"

Sage beat the water with her paddle.

"Quick, make for Whin Bay… the otters' beach. It's closer. Hurry!"

"Yes. We need to swim fast." Muir tugged at the smaller merchild's arm. "Cuan, follow me."

A wave of terror surged through him and, powered by adrenalin, Finn swam faster than he ever had in his life, following in the kayak's super-charged wake. Even so, he and Cuan were last to reach the bay, and the final few metres seemed endless, the waves pushing him in every direction but the one he needed to go.

Finn felt dizzy with relief and exhaustion when they made it to the shore. Cuan was struggling too, much less proficient on land than on water. When Finn lifted the merchild by the waist up onto a rock, he was taken aback both by how ice-cold the merchild's skin felt and by how heavy he was.

Sage had already pulled the kayak as far up the beach as she could. She approached him, breathing hard, eyes anxious. "I can't see her now – the monster."

Finn looked out to sea. The surface was relatively calm, and there was no sign of Easgann Mòr.

"It's even scarier when you can't see her." Sage shuddered. "Like when there's a huge spider on the ceiling and it scuttles out of sight."

"Yeah, and you know it's still in the room, somewhere, but you don't know exactly where."

"I'm not too worried for us. We should be okay." Sage lowered her voice. "If the tide comes right in, you and I could climb the cliff. Or we could use your phone: call the Coastguard and ask them to come and rescue us. But when the tide rises and the beach disappears, the merfolk will be in the water, whatever the danger."

Finn tugged off his swim hat and ran a hand through his hair. "Um, well. Problem one, there's no way we could climb that cliff. Look at it! It's a sheer drop onto rocks, and it's crumbling. Problem two, I didn't bring my phone. I left it in the house cause I was worried it would get wet. So, I reckon we're in as much bother as the merfolk. But the tide's low just now. We've got a few hours before Whin Bay disappears under water. Maybe Easgann Mòr will give up and move on."

He fell silent, not wanting to voice the rest of the worries swirling in his head.

Traigh, Muir and Cuan can't stay out of the water for long. Sage and I will have to keep them wet, somehow. But I'm not going back in that water. It's not that I don't want to help them, it's just that I'd prefer not to be a giant eel's lunch.

His eyes flicked back and forth, from the sea to the three merchildren huddled on the rocks. Cuan was whimpering, cuddling up to Traigh. They were clearly terrified, and Finn could hardly blame them. All three knew exactly what could happen next. It was awful to see them in such a state. Even Muir, usually so composed, kept making strange gasping sounds, as if she was struggling to breathe.

"Look, guys." He tried to keep the wobble from his voice, stay as calm as Lizzy did when Ava was having one of her wake-up tantrums. "Sage and I are going to come up with safe ways of keeping your skin from drying out, while we all think of a plan to get rid of Easgann Mòr. Okay?"

He looked at Sage for confirmation and was relieved when she nodded. But he could tell by the look in her eyes that she was scared too.

Cos she knows my original plan is going to have to be binned. Waiting and hoping that the eel will go away isn't an option – not here, where the tide covers the whole beach. We need to think of something else, and we need to think fast.

"Their tails will be drying out. We need to find water containers."

Sage was already unzipping her coat's hood. "This is waterproof. The plastic bag you brought your towel in should work too."

"Just our luck it's not raining. A rainstorm would have done the job for us."

"Look! There's Easgann Mòr!" Sage's voice was a croak of horror. "Look at the size of her!"

The gigantic eel was swimming towards Whin Bay, the bulk of her massive body just below the surface. Only the dorsal fin, running along her entire length, was visible above water. Finn guessed she was about ten metres long, although it was possible she was much bigger. She looked big enough to swallow a person whole.

Oh, heck. How are we going to get out of this mess?

As she headed towards them, Easgann Mòr seemed to slither through the waves like an adder on grass. A horrible thought occurred to Finn.

"Eels have been known to travel on land, haven't they? What if she can slither on to the rocks?" He felt panic rising in his throat.

Sage shook her head, but there was doubt in her eyes. "She looks like a conger, and conger eels are deep-sea dwellers. They live on shipwrecks and in dark, underwater caves. I'm pretty sure they don't ever move about on land." Already she'd started work, bravely standing at the sea's edge, dipping her jacket hood into the water. When he joined her and trawled his supermarket bag for life through the water, the freezing sea burnt his fingers.

"This ruddy bag's got a leak," he growled as he heaved it across the rocks and hurled it over Cuan's tail. "And this is a freaking nightmare. Why the heck did we come to Whin Bay?"

"We didn't have much choice, did we? We were being

chased by a sea monster! But it'll be okay. We can do this."

As Sage spoke, Finn glanced nervously out to sea, totally unconvinced that it was going to be okay. A horrible feeling, a conviction that things were about to get worse, was growing like algae on water.

Despite the weak winter sunshine, the air was frigid, and the thought of spending hours lugging bags of seawater across the rocks was not one bit appealing. An idea came to him.

"Why don't we fill the kayak with water? They could take turns to sit in it. If we can keep them hydrated for longer, we'll have more time to think of a decent plan."

Sage's eyes lit up. "Good idea. I'll get started."

From the rocks, Muir spoke up. "We could build a pool from some of these loose rocks, could we not, Traigh?"

Doubt it, guys. It'll leak like a sieve.

"You can have a go," Finn said brightly, thinking that at least it would give the merchildren something to do and take their minds off the terrible fate awaiting them.

Filling the kayak and then building the rock pool took both time and effort, and it was worrying to see the tide creeping slowly across the rocks as they worked. But the merchildren were amazingly good at arranging rocks to make a watertight structure, and when it was finished and half-filled, the pool was large enough for all three to dip their tails and splash water over their parched skin.

Cuan insisted on decorating the edge with tiny shells and strands of seaweed, as if it was all a fun game.

As Finn helped Sage to empty the water out of the kayak to completely fill the pool, he glanced up and caught sight of the enormous eel, turned on her side, moving in graceful, undulating movements, her slippery skin visible as humps on the surface.

Every time he ventured near the shore, he pictured that massive, snake-like body rearing up, massive jaws clamping round his face. A conger eel had attacked before: a fisherman diving off the coast of Ireland. Finn had seen the gruesome photos in the newspaper of the poor guy in hospital, a bloody chunk ripped from his cheek. And Easgann Mòr was so much bigger than the eel that fisherman had described.

They finished the task by jamming the kayak between two rocks, some distance from the incoming tide. Finn was standing beside Sage at the water's edge when the crunch of somebody moving over shingle made him turn. Little Cuan had left the rock pool and was heading across the tiny beach in search of more treasure.

"A starfish!" Cuan's squeal of delight was cut short as a large, powerful wave rolled across the shingle and engulfed the merchild.

Finn waded into the water, but Cuan was already too far away for him to grab. "The wee guy's in the sea!" he yelled.

Sage's hands flew to her mouth, smothering a gasp. "Cuan, get out the water! Hurry!"

Behind them, Traigh and Muir began to sing: a mournful, high-pitched wail, more an outpouring of grief than a song.

Panicking, Cuan whacked his tail against the surface – and Easgann Mòr noticed. The eel had been heading away from the bay in the direction of the Grey Isle, but as Finn watched, his heart thumping against his ribs, the creature reversed. Finn had only vaguely remembered that eels could swim backwards, and seeing it happening, knowing what the predator was planning, was horrifying.

"Get out of the water! Now!" Finn ran along the water's edge, waving his arms, but Cuan seemed paralysed with fear. Sage stumbled across the rocks towards the kayak.

"Help me, Finn!" she screamed.

And he remembered his own scream for help, his panic when his swim had gone wrong, his desperation as he'd screamed and swallowed seawater, his terror when he believed no one had heard him and he was about to die. It was his turn to act, but there was no time to dislodge the kayak. He'd have to swim.

Unzipping his jacket and shrugging it off, he dived into the water. It was a crazy thing to do, a sure-fire way of succumbing to the heart-stopping cold, but there was no time to acclimatise, not when Cuan was in terrible danger.

The icy temperature hit him like a brick in the face.

The merchild was near to shore but swimming in circles, panicked by the writhing humps breaking through the waves, getting closer. Finn swam up and reached out, grabbing a clump of tangled hair so wet and slimy that the tendrils almost slid out of his hand. Sage's voice seemed to come from miles away, yelling at him to hurry, to head back to shore, but it was easier said than done. He'd taken life-saving classes in the swimming pool, but nobody had told him what to do about thrashing tails or approaching monsters.

And then the nightmare became real: an enormous, dripping-wet head reared up only a metre from Cuan's tail and Finn found himself staring into large, round eyes, cold as a shark's. Easgann Mòr's jaws opened wide, revealing rows of crowded, razor-sharp teeth. Snapping forward, the eel lunged for Cuan's twisting, flapping tail. Desperate to protect the merchild, Finn kicked out as hard as he could, but his foot slid against the eel's slippery skin. As the monster's jaws clamped down on his neoprene sock, searing pain shot through Finn's body, and he screamed. As he writhed, struggling to free his trapped foot, the sock peeled off, and was left dangling in the monster's jaws. Easgann Mòr's head slid below the surface.

Doing a frantic, one-handed backstroke, gripping the terrified merchild, Finn kicked for shore. But blood was spurting from his throbbing big toe and he felt dizzy with fear.

What are Dad and Ava going to think if I don't come back? I didn't even give Mum a proper hug before she went on holiday...

Cuan was wriggling so hard that Finn kept losing his grip, but they were almost there, his uninjured foot half swimming, half slipping on the rocks below the water, nearly at the beach. Then Easgann Mòr's massive head broke the surface and those dead-fish eyes stared right through him. The monster lunged again, and Cuan let out a high-pitched, terrified wail.

17

SAGE

Pulse racing, heart pounding, Sage freed the kayak and hauled it towards the water's edge. All too aware that there was a good chance of capsizing, she stripped down to her swimming costume and slipped the buoyancy aid over her head. Adrenalin was pulsing through her so strongly that she hardly felt the cold. Behind her, Traigh and Muir's song surged and Sage swore with frustration.

Why the heck are they singing? Why aren't they trying to help?

Easgann Mòr's writhing body was at least five times longer than the kayak, and the monster was creating a swell. Sage had to use all her strength to paddle straight towards Finn and Cuan. She was within touching distance when, for the second time, the eel's head arced up out of the water.

Cuan's piercing scream shredded the scrap of courage

Sage had been clinging to, and as she stared into the monster's expressionless eyes her first instinct was to paddle backwards to the safety of the shore.

But I can't leave them to die. I need to do something!

For the first time in her life, violence seemed the only answer.

Raising her paddle in both hands, she twisted it with all her might and slapped one sturdy fibreglass blade across the eel's lower jaw.

"Leave them alone!" she yelled, twisting the paddle again so it smacked against Easgann Mòr's eye. The monster tossed her head from side to side, clearly in pain. "Get lost, you big bully!" Another mighty whack connected with the eel's teeth. "Swim, Finn! Get Cuan out of here!"

Finn kicked for shore, dragging the merchild with him.

Swinging her great head, the eel disappeared below the surface, causing waves to surge and the kayak to tip. As Sage went under, the icy cold made her gasp and panic seized her. The sea had been whipped into froth and visibility was poor, although she kept catching glimpses of Easgann Mòr's dark, snake-like form slithering down to the depths. Holding her breath, lungs bursting, Sage tried to focus. She'd practised rolls many times, just not in quite such dire circumstances.

Hips first, shoulders second, head last.

She twisted her body, moving the paddle to the correct angle, applying increasing pressure, and using her hips to try and snap the kayak back beneath her. As she swung upwards and her head finally rose out of the water, she breathed in lungfuls of fresh, tangy sea air.

The water's surface was dark-blue silk rippled by foamy ruffles, and the sun was shining. Everything looked completely, deceptively normal. There were yachts further out, but even if they came close, they would have no idea of the danger lurking underneath.

Shivering, hair dripping, Sage paddled back to the beach. When she jumped out of the kayak, her legs wobbled, weak with relief to be on land. She dragged the kayak across the rocks to where Finn was sitting. Pain was etched on his face, and his big toe was a bloody, shredded mess. Traigh and Muir were hugging the traumatised merchild and singing a song Sage had heard before. As she watched, Cuan's wailing faded to hiccups and one small fist uncurled, revealing a tiny starfish.

Then, as the merchildren kept singing, Finn's injury began to heal over. Sage saw the ripped skin knitting together and smoothing over, leaving only a small, reddish scar. The amazement on Finn's face was funny to watch: his mouth a perfect circle, eyes bulging like a frog's.

I guess he didn't believe me when I told him the merfolk's song has healing powers.

"We are sorry." Traigh's voice dripped sorrow. "It is

187

impossible to leave no trace with injuries such as these. Our powers are limited."

"Hey, no need to apologise. That was incredible! I thought my footballing days were done – not that I play much football... It doesn't even hurt any more. Sage, you're shaking like a leaf." He handed her his towel, concern in his eyes. "Sorry it's a bit damp. You were a hero, by the way."

She tried to smile but was shaking so much her facial muscles wouldn't cooperate.

"You... you were a hero too."

She made a tent of the big towel and changed underneath, glad to be out of the icy wind and relieved she'd brought a spare swimsuit, stored in a plastic pouch in the hatch. When she emerged, Finn held up her woolly hat.

"Here, put this on. You'll get a chill otherwise, without your hood."

Sage pulled the hat over her damp hair and shaded her eyes as she looked out to sea.

"It's not over yet. Easgann Mòr is still out there. What the heck are we going to do?" A thought struck her.

We need to know what worked last time.

She walked over to the merchildren and sat beside Finn on the edge of their pool.

"Muir, Traigh... A thousand years ago, when the fisherman refused to help, how did you get away from

Easgann Mòr? Maybe we could try the same again. Didn't the orca help you?"

Muir's head turned slowly towards Traigh's. "We must tell them the truth."

There was a long silence, and Sage saw reluctance in Traigh's set jaw and wary eyes. When he nodded, she sensed the merchildren had come to an unspoken decision.

Together Muir and Traigh began to speak, voices merging, words spilling.

"The legend you have been told is not the true story. The merfolk have kept a terrible secret for a thousand years… The fisherman was no coward. He agreed to help Mol when he was asked. With strength and cunning, the man succeeded in capturing the Great Eel in his fishing nets. Then Mol put a hand on the monster's body and began to sing the Song of Cianalas, to spirit her back in time, to before the Drowned Lands were lost to the sea. But as the first notes rang out, Easgann Mòr thrashed her tail and knocked the fisherman out of his boat. Determined to save the merfolk, Mol kept singing to the end. By the time he finished, the fisherman had drowned."

Sage's hand flew to her mouth, stifling a gasp of horror.

Mol let the man drown?

18

SAGE

There was a long, stunned silence, until Finn spoke.

"Wow. Your legend is actual fake news."

Swallowing, feeling slightly sick, Sage asked the question they needed to know.

"So, what happened next, after the fisherman drowned?"

"The song failed." The merchildren's voices were mournful. "It was not powerful enough. Easgann Mòr was not magically transported back in time to Cianalas. While the monster was still struggling to escape from the fisherman's nets, Mol gathered the merfolk and confessed, and we all agreed we would keep what had really happened to ourselves. We fled the north while we could and came here to the islet to start again.

"The guilt and shame of leaving the fisherman to drown have lain heavily on Mol's shoulders for a thousand years. Our failure to save him is the reason that contact with humans is so strictly forbidden. His death is our shameful secret; we are not allowed to speak his name…" Traigh and Muir paused and looked at each other before continuing. "But now is the time for change. His name was Donald Gilroy. From the very beginning merfolk vowed to do no harm, yet we allowed terrible harm to befall a human who was trying to save us."

Sage took off her hat and ran a hand through her damp, tangled hair. "You say you can do no harm, but surely if we kill this giant eel, we're causing harm to a wild creature?"

Both merfolk pursed their large lips in disapproval. "The merfolk do not wish a violent end for Easgann Mòr," they said, shock rippling in their voices. "She may be a threat to us, but she is a creature of the Undersea, just as we are."

Sage bit her lip, feeling a bit guilty about bashing the monster's face.

But I didn't have a whole lot of choice, did I? The merfolk might not believe in violence, but Easgann Mòr isn't so particular.

"Is that why you were singing when Cuan was in danger?" Finn asked. "Were you trying to get shot of the monster?"

"Yes, but the Song of Cianalas did not work for us either… We do not know why. That song is ancient, powerful magic."

"Maybe you two need to put a hand on Easgann Mòr like Mol did and sing the Song of Cianalas together. Maybe the magic from two of you at once would be powerful enough to send her back in time to her homeland," suggested Sage. "Though don't ask me how you'd manage to touch her and sing without being eaten."

"It's not the worst idea, Sage," said Finn. "But how the heck could we keep the eel still for long enough?"

Sage tried to sound upbeat and positive, although deep inside she was beginning to lose hope. "I'm sure we can figure something out."

Cuan laid the starfish gently on a pebble in the pool.

"I know where Easgann Mòr lives." The little merchild pointed out to sea, hand trembling. "When I was swimming in the Undersea I found a dark hole, and it smelled bad. I did not like the smell, so I swam away. When the eel opened its big mouth today, it had the same stinky smell! The cave smelled like her... like Easgann Mòr."

Traigh and Muir stared at Cuan. "You are sure? Where was this?"

"In the deep part of the bay. I can show you."

Sage jumped up. "I gave the monster a real thump. Broke a few teeth." Her flat, hopeless feeling had vanished as Cuan spoke, and her heart was beating fast. "She's probably in her cave right now, licking her wounds."

Muir started to clamber from the pool. "We should go there, trap her inside."

"We cannot. The humans did not bring nets, remember?" murmured Traigh.

Finn sighed. "And humans can't swim underwater."

Muir and Traigh spoke together. "There is a way we can—"

The merchildren fell silent, then turned in unison towards the sea. "We can hear the others, calling in Undersea," they explained. "They are near."

Sage jumped up just as Eilean arrived on the beach, followed by the rest of the merfolk. The air exploded with clicks and whistles, and their thrashing tails churned the shallows into froth. Mol arrived last.

"Are you safe? We saw the Great Eel in the firth and we came. Are you hurt?"

He sounded frantic. He'd seemed so cold and stern before, but now his anxious tone and furrowed brow reminded Sage of her parents.

Eilean's voice wavered and she seemed close to tears. "We saw Easgann Mòr, feared the worst and found we were less afraid of the monster than of losing our children. Traigh, all of us owe you an apology. You tried to tell us and we would not listen."

Traigh turned to Mol, his head raised high, his shoulders back, as if a load had been lifted. "If we survive this, then

193

in future Muir and I should be involved in decisions. It is not fair…"

Mol said nothing, still breathing hard from his desperate swim. Then he nodded.

"If we live, you two will join the council with the rest of us. It is time."

Sage felt frustration boiling in her chest. "Listen! Cuan believes Easgann Mòr lives in a cave out in the bay. And we think the eel's hiding there now, because I clobbered her with a paddle. So, our plan is to trap her inside her cave."

"Yup," agreed Finn. "And when the eel is trapped, we think at least two of you merfolk will need to lay their hands on her, to make the song work. But we need to hurry."

Eilean flicked her tail, splashing water across the rocks. "They are right. We must act. Now."

"But how, Eilean?" Mol gave a bitter laugh. "How do we trap Easgann Mòr?"

When we met Traigh and Muir, they asked if we had a net… Sage thought. Looking out into the firth, she saw a couple of small yachts skimming towards the open sea and a large fishing boat heading back to the harbour.

Finn had clearly spotted the boat too. "Fishermen use nets!"

"Yeah, but none of the fishing boats that come in and out of the harbour come close to Whin Bay," Sage sighed. "I guess it's too rocky here."

Again, Eilean flicked her tail. "We could easily bring the boat close enough and swim out to it. But we will not involve humankind again in our troubles. Not after what happened in the past."

"Indeed. We will not involve the fishermen." Mol's voice was stony, his eyes staring seaward.

"You wouldn't need to involve the people at all." Finn was clearly trying to keep the impatience out of his voice. "The boat's heading back to harbour. It won't be going back out today. You could borrow the net and return it before the fishermen even notice it's missing."

"And this is an actual emergency, isn't it?" added Sage, her voice shaking. "We need to do *something*."

Mol kept staring out to sea.

Then he began to sing, and, gradually, the other merfolk joined in. The tune was slow and melancholy, the language unintelligible. But Sage felt the pull of its ancient magic.

As the last notes of the merfolk's song drifted across the waves, she saw the fishing boat veer from the harbour and putter towards Whin Bay, as if tugged on an invisible rope. The reek of shellfish from the empty creels on its deck was attracting a large following of gulls. An old, disused net dangled over the boat's port side. The two fishermen onboard were standing on deck, dazed smiles on their faces.

Sage gave a low whistle. "Wow. It's like in those Greek legends, where mermaids sang to lure sailors to their deaths on the rocks."

Finn laughed. "Though in real life, the merfolk don't want to kill the sailors, just borrow their stuff."

Eilean slid from her rock. "We do not want the boat to come any closer." She gestured to two other merfolk. "Come, let us go and relieve those fishermen of their net. Quiet now."

A few minutes later, the three returned to the beach, dragging the net behind them. Sage, remembering Finn's injured toe, felt a shiver of doubt.

"Won't the eel be able to bite through that?"

"Eels have very poor eyesight, though it will be necessary to strike quickly, while she is confused," Eilean explained. She turned to the smallest merchild. "Cuan, you must be brave now and lead the way to Easgann Mòr's lair."

Cuan nodded, but Sage noticed his little pointed chin wobble.

They're all scared, but they're being so brave. If only Finn and I could swim underwater! We could help hold the net. We're not going to be any use on land…

It appeared Finn was thinking the same.

"Look, I'm pure rubbish at singing and I don't know the ruddy song. But if there's any way I can help in the water, I'm willing. I'm a good swimmer."

Mol bared his sharp teeth.

"The Song of the Undersea is not one we have needed to use since the end of the Land Time. It is not one I plan to use again. We cannot risk causing harm."

Eilean's voice rippled, as soothing as Mol's was harsh. "We can dilute its effects. It will not be permanent; instead, it will give the children greater strength and let them hold their breath until their task is done. It does make sense, Mol. They can be of no help to us here, and we will need all our voices if the Song of Cianalas is to work."

"It's not as if you'd be doing it with bad intentions." Sage voice trembled, a mix of fear and excitement. "You're trying to keep the merfolk safe. And Finn and I are willing to take the risk."

Finn shook his head. "Don't be daft, Sage! You can't come. You're not wearing a wetsuit. You'll get hypothermia."

"The song provides protection from the cold." Mol looked up at the gulls still wheeling above them. "We cannot waste any more time." He gestured towards the merfolk clustered on the rocks. "When the human children are ready, Eilean and I will sing the Song of the Undersea, so they can access our world. Then, when Cuan gives the word, together we will sing the Song of Cianalas, with all the combined strength in our lungs."

He turned to Traigh and Muir, his eyes brimming. "I failed a thousand years ago, but together, your touch might have more powerful magic. And you may remind Easgann Mòr that she was young once too, and can be so again. Traigh and Muir, you will accompany the human children to the eel's lair. Cuan, you will show them the way."

There was a gasp of horror from the adult merfolk, but Mol put up a webbed hand to hush them. "If the plan goes wrong, Cuan will swim back to let us know, and we will go to their rescue."

The two merchildren spoke in unison. "It will not go wrong. We will get rid of Easgann Mòr forever."

Traigh's gaze was steady, his shoulders back. He looked proud, but Sage noticed his hands were trembling, and she wondered if he believed his own words.

19

FINN

Excitement, spiked with terror, exploded inside Finn.

OMG! They're going to turn me into freaking Aquaman!

Sage went over to the kayak and returned with a large black torch, which she handed to him.

"You're the faster swimmer, so do you want to take this? It'll be dark down there and I want to see where we're going."

As he took the torch, she grinned at him, excitement dancing in her eyes. "This is *unreal*! We're going to be temporary merfolk!"

After removing their warm outer layers, Sage and Finn waded into the sea. As Traigh, Muir and Cuan plunged underwater, pulling the net behind them, Finn's courage faltered, the memory of his near drowning making him shudder.

Beside him, Sage shivered in her thin swimsuit, her skin bluish and goosepimpled.

199

Mol's wrong. She's going to get hypothermia. Dad freaks out about the ice milers. He'd go ballistic about this plan.

"This is crazy," he grumbled. "We should go home, Sage. What the heck were we thinking?"

Then Eilean and Mol began to sing. Finn couldn't understand a single word, but he breathed in the song and let courage fill his lungs.

The panic dissolved and was replaced by a kind of euphoria, rushing through his bloodstream, warming him, filling his brain with self-belief.

I can do this. I can hold my breath underwater for as long as it takes.

He dived, and Sage followed.

Under the waves, out of the wind, the cold didn't feel as biting. In fact, the faster Finn swam the warmer he became, and Sage didn't seem to be suffering either as she followed the others down into the Undersea. The deeper they went, the dimmer and greener the light gleamed, and the stranger the environment became. As Finn swam through a strange, swaying forest of seaweed, he passed spiky pink sea urchins and scuttling hermit crabs. Spotlit in the torch beam, he saw the pale, drifting tentacles of a cluster of anemones.

Sage swam beside him, using strong, even strokes, her long dark hair trailing like weed. Occasionally she turned to smile at him, as if she too was struggling to believe that this was actually happening. Once or twice she slowed, to point out the weird and wonderful creatures they passed: a scallop emerging from the sand and bouncing across the seafloor; a small squat lobster peering from the crevice of a rock, its claws snapping aggressively.

Traigh and Muir kept doubling back, encouraging the children to keep up. Cuan enjoyed showing off his seal-like acrobatic skills, spinning and twirling in the water as if it was all a wonderful game. In their natural element, the merfolk's skin took on a greenish tinge, like verdigris on copper, and their hair, limp and straggly on land, became beautiful amber and gleaming emerald strands rippling in the currents. Finn wished with all his heart he was as strong and confident underwater as the merchildren.

The Undersea was so different, so fascinating, it was almost possible to forget why they were down there.

As Cuan's tail flicked against the sea floor, a cloud of silt obscured the view. Finn nearly crashed into Traigh and Muir, who'd stopped and were clicking in their strange Undersea language. Finn's euphoria dissolved, replaced by a chill of fear.

We're here. We've reached the cave.

Gradually the murk cleared, and Finn realised that the dark hole Cuan had described wasn't a cave at all.

Ahead, half-buried in silt, lay the rusting, barnacle-encrusted hull of a wrecked cargo steamer. On its crumbling deck, anemones swayed in the tidal current, clustering on the collapsed remains of the foremast.

Cuan pointed towards a jagged hole in the ship's starboard side, and Traigh and Muir swam nearer, dragging the net.

Sage turned to Finn. Speech was impossible, but she reached out and squeezed his hand.

Muir gestured at Cuan, who was fidgety with nerves, to stay where he was. Each holding a corner of the net, Sage, Finn, Traigh and Muir swam using steady, cautious strokes. As they got nearer they stopped kicking, anxious to get into a good position and desperate not to make any unnecessary movements that might attract the eel's attention.

Finn couldn't help sneaking glances at the gaping hole in the ship's side. His chest tightened and the urge to take a breath grew with his anxiety.

If the eel attacks, we won't stand a chance.

And as soon as they reached the ship, his fears were realised.

From the dark hole, the monster's head emerged, jaws gaping, and she launched herself forward. Her teeth clamped down on Muir's tail and blood tinged the water pink. Oblivious to the merchild's frantic clicks and squeals, the eel went into reverse, dragging Muir into her lair.

No, you don't! Let go!

202

Taking the torch in both hands, Finn focused the beam directly in the eel's eyes. Confused, she let go of her prey, and Muir's tail flicked hard against the sea floor, sending clouds of silt flying. But Finn could see Easgann Mòr was powering up to strike again, preparing to propel her massive body out into the open water, where she'd be free to lash out with both her jaws and her massive tail.

He gestured wildly, hoping the others would understand.

Go, Cuan! Tell the merfolk to start singing. We'll get the net ready. Now!

But everyone seemed to know already what they had to do. Cuan was speeding towards Whin Bay. Sage was tugging the fishing net into position, grasping it so tightly her knuckles looked bone-white in the semi-darkness. Despite her injury, Muir was helping Traigh to hold the net tightly across the opening. Traigh even managed to hook a corner over a piece of the jagged metal on the torn hull, leaving both his hands free. While Finn and the others clung desperately to the net, the eel launched herself forward. She hit the mesh with a terrifying thud – the net held! – and then retreated.

It'll be back – and stronger next time.

Traigh had positioned himself right in front of the net, but for some unfathomable reason he was thrashing around, making the corners even harder to grip.

What's the daft bampot doing?

203

But then it dawned on Finn: Traigh's tail had become trapped in the mesh, and no matter how hard he pulled he couldn't release it. If any of the others tried to help, they would have to let go of their corner – and the eel would escape and turn on them all. Poor Muir was already weakening, eyes glazed with pain, blood pouring from her wounded tail.

Finn felt panic rising. His chest felt tight, as if it were about to explode.

I need to get out of here. I need to breathe.

Then Sage kicked – hard. Still gripping with both hands, her bare foot swung at the net again and again, making it flex. Desperate, Traigh tugged and tugged until finally the end of his tail sprang free, just as the eel's jaws snapped shut on the mesh.

She's going to bite through the net!

But bravely, Traigh pressed both hands on the side of the creature's closed mouth. Struggling to keep her corner of the net tight, Muir stretched out her free hand, reached through the mesh and pressed it to the eel's side.

And then the singing started, rolling towards them in an underwater wave. The Song of Cianalas was different from the merfolk's other songs: deeper, more melodious, and full of a desperate longing for home that hurt Finn's heart.

Easgann Mòr stopped snapping at the net and stilled. As Finn watched, mesmerised, the old ship began to glow in the dim, grey-green light of the Undersea. On the deck, the anemones' waving tentacles emitted an iridescent gleam and the barnacles on the hull turned neon-blue. The huge eel's skin glistened like mercury, shimmered into a million tiny droplets, and suddenly she vanished, back in time to Cianalas.

Then the brightness faded and the ship became a rusting wreck once more.

20

SAGE

There was no time for celebrations. Muir was writhing in pain, and Sage felt her lungs were about to explode. Swimming with all his power, Traigh dragged Muir back towards Whin Bay, while Finn and Sage swam upwards, desperate for air. When she reached the surface, Sage sucked in great mouthfuls of oxygen and held her face up to the sunlight, filled with relief at being able to breathe normally again. It felt very different being in the sea now she knew the monster had gone.

She treaded water and grinned at Finn. "We did it! Can you believe we were underwater for that long? It was magic, wasn't it? Did you see how the shipwreck glowed? Did you see Easgann Mòr disappear?" She paused and began to shiver. "It's freaking freezing!"

Finn grabbed her arm. "Yeah, you should be dead by now, really. Let's get back to shore before the song wears off completely, and get warmed up. Race you!"

The waters of Whin Bay were brimming with merfolk keen to ease the pain of their dried, cracked skin now that the sea was safe. A few were gathered around Mol, who was singing softly to Muir, trying to heal her injury. The terrible gash was knitting together, though she would be left with a long, jagged scar.

When they'd dried their hair and put on their jackets, Finn and Sage stood and watched the merfolk. Already, Muir had returned to the water, earnestly practising her dives. Sage was still shivering, her shoulders sagging with tiredness and relief.

"Sadness seems to cling to them, doesn't it?" Finn kept his voice low, clearly not wanting his words to carry on the breeze. "Even after all this, the merfolk's faces are tripping them." He paused. "Actually, that phrase was one of my gran's favourites, and my dad has been using it a lot lately. *Oi, Finn, your face is tripping you. Cheer up!* He gave Sage a rueful smile. "But you can't just cheer up to order can you? You need to have a reason. Maybe the merfolk don't have one."

Sage chose her words carefully. "I feel sorry for them. Change is hard." She gave him a sideways glance and saw a flush creep up his neck.

Then he laughed. "Oh, I don't know. It would be pretty amazing to be able to swim like an Olympian."

"Yes, but having a fishtail would take a lot of getting used to." She paused. "Maybe the merfolk would be happier if they accepted that they can't go back to how things were, way back in the Land Time, but they can make the most of how things *are*."

Finn coughed and wouldn't catch her eye.

"And maybe now they're no longer afraid," she mused, "now that Easgann Mòr is no longer a threat, they'll be able to relax and start to enjoy life more." She gave his sleeve a gentle tug. "Anyway, we've done our bit. It's time to go home."

As they hauled the kayak across the beach, Muir and Traigh bobbed up out of the waves.

Muir spoke first, in her odd, bubbling voice. "We are very grateful to you. We have been adrift and afraid for thousands of years, but now we can make a real home, on our islet here in the firth."

Traigh flicked his hair, spun round in the water. "Thanks to you, we have been able to prove to the others that we have both sense and courage."

He already seems different, Sage thought. *More confident. Almost happy.*

Muir held up a familiar object.

"Mol says you must keep this. Inside, there are gifts for you both, with the merfolk's grateful, heartfelt thanks. Wear them, and if you are ever in trouble at sea, we merfolk will know it and come to your aid."

When Sage held out her hand to take the shell box, she touched Muir's skin and, strangely, didn't feel the same discomfort as before. Maybe it was because Sage was so cold and wet, but this time there didn't appear to be any difference between them.

"Thank you," Sage whispered. "Whatever's inside, I'll treasure it. Always." She smiled at the merchildren. "Take care of those gorgeous otters."

"We will... Perhaps we can learn from them too, and have some fun."

The merchildren were almost completely underwater, their hair drifting on the waves, and sadness swept over Sage, knowing that it was over, and she might never see them again.

Muir's lips curved, in a ghost of a smile.

"If all human children are like you two, there is hope for the creatures of the Undersea."

The journey back only took ten minutes, both children propelled along by the merchildren, who vanished underwater before they had the chance to say goodbye.

While Finn was getting changed on the beach beneath the castle, Sage emptied water from the kayak and clipped the paddle back in place. And as she worked, she came to a decision.

I can't hold on to it any longer. It's not mine.

"I'm going to leave the kayak out here in the open." She bit her lip, trying to stop the tears that were nipping her eyes. "Hopefully its rightful owner will find it."

Finn gave her a sympathetic glance. "Good call, but tough…" He held up his sodden wetsuit. "At least you can abandon the evidence of your crime. I've got to try and sneak this wetsuit, minus an expensive sock, and this soaking towel, back into the house again without anyone noticing. What are my chances?"

Sage laughed. "I reckon you'll manage it. And I also reckon it's time to go. My parents – and your dad – will be on their way back from the final planning meeting, so we'd better be there to console them or celebrate."

She pulled the shell box from her pocket.

"Before we say goodbye, let's open this box, shall we? See what's inside."

"Who bets it's more seaweed?"

But it wasn't seaweed. As the top half of the cockle shell sprang open, Sage gasped. Nestled inside were two small discs of mother-of-pearl threaded onto thin silver chains. Blues and greens swirled across the surface of the discs, and they glistened like fish scales in the sunlight.

"Wow. Merfolk treasure!" She fastened hers round her neck. "It's so beautiful. I'm going to wear mine always."

Finn fastened his own. "I'll wear mine too. You should keep the box."

Sage shook her head. It was tempting, but it wouldn't do.

If Zara finds it, she might wonder…

"Thanks, but no. I'm going to have enough bother explaining the necklace to my mums. You have it."

He was silent for a moment. "Thanks. I think I might give it to my stepmother. I've bought my mum a nice present already, but I haven't got anything for Lizzy. I didn't get her anything on purpose, and that seems a bit spiteful now. I think she'll really like this." He shoved the shell in his pocket and gave a careless shrug. "Though if she doesn't, tough luck. I'm not spending actual money on her."

"Yeah, best not go too far, too soon." Sage grinned, wishing this wasn't the end, that somehow the two of them could stay friends. "Aw, I'll miss your cheery smile and upbeat chat. I hope you have a fab Christmas, Finn. If you're ever in Cornwall…"

Finn smiled, a genuinely happy smile that made his eyes shine. It was lovely to see, like the sun peeking from behind a dark raincloud.

"Are you kidding? My dad and I go to Port Isaac for a week every August. It's a fab place for wild swimming."

Sage had just arrived at the entrance to Cliff Lodges when the bus stopped and her parents and Taj got out.

Taj was dancing around, excitement dancing in his eyes. "We won, Sage! The planning guys said a big fat no to Mr McPherson. He's a total loser!"

Zara tsked disapprovingly. "Taj, dear, we should always be gracious, both in defeat and in victory." But her eyes glowed with delight, and Sage reckoned she'd be punching the air and yelling too if Taj wasn't around.

"That's great. It really is." And it was, for her family, and for the other protestors, but she couldn't help feeling a twinge of sympathy for Finn's dad, and she hoped it wouldn't spoil their Christmas. "Sorry I couldn't be at the meeting. Like I said in my note, I was meeting up with my friend."

Kate put an arm round her shoulders and drew her into a hug. "You don't need to apologise, lovely girl. Just because Zara and I throw ourselves into fighting for causes, it doesn't mean you have to. You do know that, don't you? You're old enough to decide for yourself. We won't mind at all."

They'd never said that before, either of them. Maybe they'd sensed her increasing reluctance to join in their campaigns. It felt nice to know they realised she was growing up and that she was old enough to make her own decisions.

"Though maybe we should get her a mobile phone, so we can check where she is," muttered Zara over the top of Sage's head as they all walked together, arm in arm, back up to the lodge. "Save any worry."

"Great plan!" Sage didn't even try to pretend she hadn't heard, or that a phone didn't matter to her. Everybody had one. She needed a phone, particularly if she was going to message Finn to chat, and to arrange their meet-up in the summer – and to keep in touch with the new friends she was determined to make in Cornwall. After all, now she had one good friend, making more seemed perfectly doable. "It could be an after-Christmas present."

Taj ran in a circle, too excited to walk in a straight line. "We won! We beat the bully!"

She grinned at him. "Yeah, one down, one to go."

"What are you two on about?" sighed Zara. "And Sage, why is your hair damp? Has it been raining here?"

Sage wrapped her arms round her mother and gave her another massive hug. "If it rained, I didn't notice. Zara, is the place we're moving to anywhere near Port Isaac?"

"Not far away. A few miles, I think."

"Excellent. I've heard it's really nice."

Kate beamed at her. "I'm so glad you're sounding more positive about the move, because we're thinking of heading there sooner rather than later, so you can start your new school in January. What do you think about that plan?"

Sage nodded. "Sounds good to me. And I think Taj will be delighted." She paused, and watched her brother zooming along the path, arms outstretched. "There's something I need to tell you about Taj…"

21

FINN

As soon as Finn came downstairs the following morning, Ava leapt from the couch and threw her arms round his waist. "It's Christmas Eve! Santa's coming tonight! Are you excited, Finn? Are you?"

He grinned, not even having to fake enthusiasm.

I saved the merfolk and survived a monster eel attack. Christmas is the icing on the cake.

"I sure am. Can't wait to see what Santa brings. We'd better hang up our stockings, hadn't we?"

Ava rolled her eyes. "Lizzy and me did that ages ago! Didn't you even notice?" She was right. Two red felt stockings were hanging from the banisters.

"That one's mine – the one with the snowman, cos I like snowmen. And the one with Santa is yours, cos Father Christmas and Finn both start with F."

"Right. Good thinking."

"Any ideas on what to do today?" Lizzy smiled at him, and he smiled back, feeling lighter, as if he'd had weights tied to his body and they'd been taken away. "If it's okay," she continued, "I'd like to do something that will cheer up your dad. He's still not sure he did the right thing yesterday, even though I've told him he's a hero."

Dad did something heroic? Really?

Finn turned to his father. "All you said last night was that the planners turned down the development."

Finn's father grimaced and rubbed at his unshaven chin. "Yeah, well, that was my doing, at least according to McPherson. It wasn't a great move financially, but I've got plenty of other work. We won't starve."

"What happened, Dad?"

His father took a large swig of coffee and sighed. "Well, after you mentioned you'd seen otters, I got in touch with the Scottish Wildlife Trust and they confirmed that yes, there are definitely otters in the local area. So, at the meeting, I thought it was only right to let the planning committee know. McPherson was not a happy man. To tell the truth, he was spitting teeth, particularly when the committee went on to turn down the planning application. I got a hundred per cent of the blame."

Finn reached over and ruffled his dad's thinning hair. "Wow... Mr McPherson might hate your guts, but I agree with Lizzy. You're a hero, Dad."

216

As they ate breakfast, an idea popped into his head. After all, it was a beautiful day, with crisp winter sunshine and a calm sea.

"Why don't we take the Wayfarer out and go around to Whin Bay, where I saw the otters?" He paused, anxious not to land himself in trouble. "When I was running along the clifftop, I mean. We'd get a much better view from the shore."

Later, as they sailed towards Whin Bay, the sea breeze was ice cold, and though they were all wrapped up well and wearing life jackets, he had a sneaking suspicion that Lizzy and Dad weren't loving his plan. When they tied up the boat, leaving it bobbing in the sea, and clambered over the slippery rocks, Lizzy was shivering and Dad's knotted eyebrows suggested he was wondering why he'd swapped his luxury holiday house for a dank, isolated cove. Only Ava fizzed with enthusiasm, especially when she found the merchildren's rock pool.

"Lizzy, look at this! It's so pretty!"

Lizzy dutifully admired the pool, now an untidy mess of scattered shells and trailing seaweed strands. Finn looked for Cuan's starfish, but it had vanished with the tide.

Alerted by high-pitched squeaks, Finn peered over the top of the rock and waved his family over. "Hey, look who's here!"

The three young otters were scampering across the stones, chasing each other, turning and twisting, their sleek coats gleaming in the sunshine. Their mother was sunning herself on a large rock, oblivious to the cold, her long, flat tail curled around her body.

"Oh, look at them. Aren't they adorable!" Lizzy's voice was breathy with excitement. Before, he'd have shuddered, believed she was pretending. But now he knew she wasn't a fake, her enthusiasm no longer made his teeth itch. And she was absolutely right: the otters were adorable.

His dad had a big, sappy grin on his face. He put his arm round Lizzy's shoulders. "What beautiful animals. You were right, Lizzy. This place is perfect, just as it is."

Finn rolled his eyes and picked Ava up so she could get a better view. "Give it a rest, guys. No physical affection in front of us kids. It's deeply gross."

Dad laughed and ruffled his hair. "As your gran used to say, you're a cheeky so-and-so."

When they headed back to Dunlyre, Finn stared at the distant Grey Isle, picturing the merfolk: scraping limpets, flicking their tails in the rock pools, and singing sad songs that yearned for the past, while little Cuan cavorted in the water, clicking and whistling like a dolphin, happy as those otters. He hoped the merchild would stay happy, because, though it was hard to admit it, happiness felt pretty good.

Christmas Day was better than he'd imagined. He got some excellent presents from Dad and Lizzy, and Lizzy adored the shell box. All day she kept fiddling with it, opening it up, holding it up to the light and exclaiming over the beautiful colours inside.

"Where on earth did you get it, Finn? It's absolutely gorgeous!"

He could hardly tell her the truth. 'It's from the Undersea' would have taken a lot of explaining. But he was glad she liked it, all the same.

About midday, Mum phoned to wish him a merry Christmas.

"I'm missing you and Avie like crazy. Can't wait to get home and give you both a massive hug. And I can't wait to see your face when you unwrap the present I've got waiting for you back at home!" She laughed. "Oh, I'm rubbish at keeping secrets. I need to tell you before I burst! I've got you a surfboard. I thought you could learn when you go to Port Isaac in the summer with your dad. He wants to take you for a fortnight this year, instead of one week. Hope that's okay."

"Yeah, it's great. Really great. Thanks, Mum... Love you."

He heard an intake of breath, and when his mum spoke she sounded choked up, as if she had a heavy cold. "I love you too, Finn."

But the most magical moments happened when he took Ava out for a walk in the late afternoon, while Dad and Lizzy finished making Christmas dinner. He left the house with strict orders not to go near the cliffs, or the main road, or the sea, which didn't really leave anywhere except downhill towards the harbour, past houses twinkling with coloured lights. Frost glittered on the pavements and the cold fogged their breath. Ava skipped along beside him, swishing her new lightsaber, jacket zipped over her sparkly Cinderella costume.

"Santa didn't bring a real live unicorn," she said cheerfully. "But I don't mind. I like the fluffy one you got me best. She's called Snuggles."

"Good name. And yeah, Lizzy was right. No live animals in Santa's sack. It wouldn't be kind, would it?"

As they reached the harbour, he spotted a familiar figure in a too-big purple coat. Sage was walking along the beach, accompanied by a small boy in a pink woolly hat.

We'll stay back from the sea. And we'll only be five minutes.

When he yelled her name, Sage turned and waited until he joined her on the rocks.

"Finn, good to see you! Merry Christmas! Hi, you must be Ava… This is my brother Taj."

"Nice hat. My jacket matches." Ava waved her lightsaber. "Want to play pirates?"

Taj grinned, revealing all the gaps in his teeth, and

tugged a piece of driftwood from a pile of kelp. "Yup. Here's my sword."

"Do *not* bash Ava with that thing," Sage ordered.

Ava gave her a withering look. "We're not fighting each other, silly. We're fighting an alien sea monster."

"Yeah, an alien sea monster from space!" yelled Taj, leaping onto a rock. "Get on the ship, quick! It's heading straight for us!"

As the sun dipped lower, Finn and Sage sat on a rock talking about everything that had happened, working out how they would keep in touch.

"We've been through something incredible, and you're the only person I'll ever be able to talk to about it." There was a slight wobble in Sage's voice.

"Yeah, so we *have* to stay friends, don't we? We'll meet up in summer, and who knows what we'll find? There are all sorts of legends about Cornwall. Wouldn't it be great if our merfolk aren't as alone as they think…"

"Yeah, I'm definitely up for that. Looks like Taj and Ava would have fun hanging out too." Sage smiled. "Look, we need to go. My mums are cooking cranberry and lentil bake, and it'll be ready soon." She got to her feet. "Bye Finn. It's been an adventure."

"Bye, Sage. Thanks for everything. Merry Christmas."

As he stood up, she gave him a massive hug. "And a happy new year when it comes, pal."

Finn had been keeping a close eye on Ava, in case she went too close to the water – he'd had more than enough near-drowning drama for one week. But both children had stayed well away from the encroaching waves. Instead, they'd clambered on the rocks, battling the invisible alien sea monster, and were now exploring a brackish rock pool. He was about to tell Ava it was time to go when he heard her comparing the pool to the one she'd discovered yesterday.

"We sailed in our ship to Finn's Bay and I found a mermaid pool, full to bits with treasure," she insisted. "Like silver shells and cockle spells."

Taj nodded enthusiastically. "I 'spect it was merfolk treasure. I've seen real live merfolk, you know." He straightened up and gazed out to sea. "Look! There they are! Sage, see! I told you so!"

Following Taj's pointed finger, Finn and Sage turned towards the horizon, where the sun was sinking into a sea of molten gold, and two distant fishtailed figures splashed in the waves.

MERFOLK

Merfolk have appeared in myths and legends for thousands of years.

 Ancient Syrian goddess Atargis dived into a lake, hoping to be transformed into a fish – but only her bottom half changed. She is now known as the first mermaid.

 Fifty Ancient Greek sea nymphs called the Nereids were kind to sailors and fishermen. One of the Nereids was the mother of the god Triton, a merman.

 In Japanese mythology, water demons called the Kappa live in rivers and lakes and look more reptile than human, with tortoise shells on their backs and scaly skin.

 Christopher Columbus claimed he spotted mermaids when he was exploring the Caribbean. According to his log, he saw "three mermaids, that came very high up out of the sea; but they were not so beautiful as they are depicted". It's possible that these 'mermaids' were actually manatees!

 In Victorian times, fake mermaids often appeared in exhibitions and circuses. P.T. Barnum advertised a mermaid in his famous show. It had the body, head and limbs of a monkey, attached to the bottom part of a large fish.

Merrows in Irish folklore are merfolk with green-tinged skin, webbed fingers, fishtails and seaweed-green hair.

 In Scottish folklore, the Ceasg (Kee-ask) has the upper half of a beautiful woman and the tail of a salmon. If she is captured, she will grant three wishes.

 Scottish mythological selkies can take seal or human form. In many stories, a man steals and hides a selkie's skin. The selkie longs to go home to the sea, and when at last she finds her seal skin, she will immediately return.

 In Scottish folklore, the Blue Men of the Minch summon storms to sink boats. Sometimes they swim up to ships and challenge the crew. If the sailors fail the challenge, the Blue Men capsize their boat.

 You can spot merfolk all over Scotland – even on dry land! There is a mermaid sculpted on the King's Fountain in Linlithgow Palace, built by King James V in 1538. The Ross Fountain in Princes Street Gardens, Edinburgh, has mermaid and merchildren statues. On a rock by the sea in Balintore, Easter Ross, sits a bronze statue called the Mermaid of the North. At high tide, the water covers her tail.

GLOSSARY

a' – all
auld – old
aye – yes
bahookie – bottom
bampot – idiot
bog off – go away, get lost
bloomin' – very
daft – silly, stupid
eejit – idiot
Firth of Clyde – inlet of the River Clyde, on the west coast of Scotland, and the deepest coastal waters in the British Isles
flaming – very
guff – nonsense
guid – good
lad – boy
loch – lake
lummox – clumsy idiot
manky – dirty
mince – garbage, terrible
minging – disgusting
ned – delinquent (offensive)
no' – not
numpty – idiot

o' – of
och – oh
ragin' – angry
skelp – hit
so and so – a person who is being annoying (sometimes used affectionately)
tae – to or too
telt – told
thrawn – stubborn
tumshie – literally a turnip, but also used affectionately to mean a daft person
wee – small, and also pee
'What's fur ye wull no' go by ye' – 'What's for you will not go by you' (Scottish saying meaning you won't miss out on something that's meant to be)
windaes – windows
ye – you
yon – that

ALSO BY LINDSAY LITTLESON

Read an extract!

1

Lewis

Rhona peered over the edge of the cliff, grinning like a gargoyle. Far below, Lewis dangled in his harness, legs kicking, frantic with fear.

"You were meant to hold on to the rocks!" she called, her voice choked with laughter. "You weren't supposed to let go!"

"It isn't funny," he muttered. "Shut up, shut up, shut up."

Terror was making his guts clench, his throat tighten. His palms were so clammy they slid on the rope. This was the polar opposite of funny.

He was making a fool of himself, as he'd known he would. His list of fails was getting longer. He was rubbish at rugby, clueless at kayaking, a failure at football and now, brand new to the list, abysmal at abseiling. And that was the edited version, not the complete list. Not even close.

The instructor on the ground was yelling instructions, but he might as well have been speaking in Mandarin, like Lewis's mother when she chatted on the phone to Grandpa in his Beijing flat. Lewis could only make out every fifth word, then or now.

He was too far up, a dizzying, terrifying distance from Earth. If his harness broke, he'd plummet head first onto rocks. He could imagine the sickening crack as his neck snapped on impact, his skull crushed, brains oozing from under the helmet, gloopy as frogspawn.

That was the one thing Lewis excelled at: imagining worst-case scenarios.

It was no struggle to picture his mother's face when she got the phone call telling her the tragic news; he could hear her breaking down, distraught, sobbing at his funeral. "My poor boy! He had his whole life ahead of him. I should never have let him go. Why was I so selfish?" A major downside of being dead would be his inability to answer back, to remind her that he'd told her many times that he didn't want to go on the trip, and she hadn't listened, that she'd never listened.

"Oi! Lewis! You look like ma granny's soap on a rope!"

The vision dissolved and Lewis was dragged back to real life, dangling from a cliff face, jagged rocks below, helpless as an upended beetle. Imagining his own funeral had been more fun.

"Belt up, Rhona. It's not funny." Lewis had been aiming for irritated, but instead his words flew out as squawks of panic. Rhona burst out laughing.

"You should see it from up here! It really is funny. It's bloomin' hysterical."

Scott leant over the cliff edge and waved a gloved hand. "Right, Lewis! No worries! We're bringing you down!"

The rope moved and Lewis was mortified to hear a whimper of terror that could only be his. Slowly, the rope started to descend and his body began to spin, like a hanged corpse. Lewis opened his eyes, saw jutting black rocks and squeezed them shut again. But the spinning rope was making him so dizzy he was scared he might spew, so he prised his eyes open and focused on the horizon: jagged mountains, a vast expanse of bleak moorland.

And then he saw it.

At first, it was a dark smudge, far in the distance. The smudge was moving fast, tracing a path across the moor, arcing like a shooting star across the sky. As it came nearer, he could see it was an animal: huge, broad-backed, long-legged.

Lewis blinked, unable to believe his eyes, which wasn't unreasonable: his eyesight was dodgy and his glasses were tucked inside his rucksack. Oblivious to the swinging rope, he kept staring; even Rhona's raucous voice faded into the background.

It couldn't be. Lewis blinked again, trying to clear his vision, remove what could only be a mirage.

Though that can't be right, can it? Mirages happen in deserts and there are no deserts in Scotland, it's too wet. Although on second thoughts, Eastgate's a desert. No cinema, no theatre, no museums. It doesn't even have a Costa. All you can do in Eastgate is get a haircut, buy booze or place a bet… Right, stop havering… Need to focus. There isn't anything weird going on. Nothing weird at all. Everything's fine.

But when he stopped blinking frantically and looked again, he could still see it. Across the moor galloped a huge dark beast, a heavily muscled horse with a gleaming, rippling black mane. The animal reared up, its hooves cutting the sky and its silken tail streaming like a banner. Its spiralled horn glinted in the sun.

Lewis blinked again. But the animal didn't vanish. He was still staring at a unicorn.

It has to be a dream. Or maybe I've died of fear.

"Hey, guys. Keep the area clear, will you?" yelled Scott. "I need to bring Lewis down safely!"

It dawned on Lewis then that he couldn't possibly be dead. He was still hanging from the rope, still cringing with shame.

When his heels scraped against rock he wanted to weep with relief, but the nightmare wasn't over.

"I bet it won't be so bad next time," said Rhona, his best

pal in the world – let's face it, his only pal in the world.

She craned her neck upwards and waved her arms like wind turbines. "Can I go again, Scott?" she bawled. "And can Lewis have another go an' aw?"

Lewis fished around in his brain for something to say, but his mind seemed to have been ambushed by unicorns. An enormous herd of unicorns was galloping around in his head, snorting, neighing, kicking their hooves. He felt his face flush, and he turned away from her, focused on hauling his rucksack onto his shoulders.

"Give over, will you?" he muttered.

One thing was for sure, he couldn't tell her that while he'd been swinging from that rope he'd imagined he'd seen a unicorn. She'd think he had lost his mind. He was already the odd one out at school, the solitary freak who always had his nose in a book. Now he was the freak who spotted unicorns. When he closed his eyes, he could see the unicorn again: powerful and magnificent, roaming free across the moor.

The story continues in

GUARDIANS
OF THE WILD
UNICORNS

PRAISE FOR LINDSAY LITTLESON

GUARDIANS OF THE WILD UNICORNS:

'An adventure tale that melds the real and the fantastic with warmth and humour.'
– *The Herald*

'Suffused with genuinely funny moments, as well as a real sense of jeopardy.'
– *BookTrust*

'A fantastically enchanting and exciting adventure story that absolutely grips you from the first page.'
– *Unicorns and Kelpies*

'The quality of writing throughout is wonderful... This is Littleson's most assured work yet.'
– *John O'Groats Journal*

'Wonderfully atmospheric and mythical with a conservation undercurrent alongside complex family issues. Children will be enthralled by these magnificently wild unicorns.'
– *South Wales Evening Post*

'Lindsay Littleson has been bold enough to strip away the sparkle and return the unicorn to its status as a mythical beast.'
– *West Coast Review*

'It's magical, but also very real and gritty.'
– *Bookwitch*

'A new and utterly inventive take on the unicorn myth,
with not a splinter of sparkle in sight.
Entertaining and atmospheric.'
– *Inverness Courier*

'A fantastic story.'
– *Armadillo*

'[The] descriptions feel so authentic that they have
the reader convinced that they too, might encounter a
unicorn on a stormy Highland night.'
– *Roaring Reads*

THE LILY MCLEAN SERIES:

'Believable, authentic characters in a story
that never lags. Very likable!'
– *Youth Services Book Review*

'Funny, beautifully written, original and finally
extremely moving, this is young teen fiction at its best.'
– *Carousel*

'A perfect summer story all about families, friends and
well some very weird happenings.'
– *Armadillo*

'A fun and quirky read, ideal for fans of
Jacqueline Wilson and Sarah Webb.'
– *Children's Books Ireland*

Also by Lindsay Littleson

Reasons why this is the BEST summer ever:

⭐ I get a FREE holiday without my moany teenage sister or my annoying little brothers.

⭐ I get to miss my primary school Leavers' Dance and avoid wearing my sister's ghastly hand-me-down dress!

Reasons why this is the WORST summer ever:

⭐ Marshmallow ice cream can't fix everything.

⭐ I'm hearing a voice, and either I'm being haunted or I'm going crazy. And I don't know which is worse...

 Also available as an eBook

DiscoverKelpies.co.uk

Things that COULD go wrong at high school:

⭐ I get lost. (Let's be honest, this WILL happen...)

⭐ Someone finds out about the psychic thing. (Who wants to be friends with a girl who hears voices?)

Things that ARE going wrong at high school:

⭐ Someone is telling lies about my best friend.

⭐ The creepy psychic stuff might be the only way to help my sister...

 Also available as an eBook

DiscoverKelpies.co.uk

ABOUT THE AUTHOR

Lindsay Littleson is an award-winning children's author from Glasgow, Scotland. Her books include *Guardians of the Wild Unicorns*, *The Mixed-Up Summer of Lily McLean*, and *The Awkward Autumn of Lily McLean*.

Inspired by many happy years as a primary school teacher, Lindsay's books are full of believable characters, authentic dialogue and just a bit of magic. They are often set in real-life places in Scotland, including Arran, Cumbrae and Ayrshire. She has four grown-up children, and currently lives in Renfrewshire with her husband and their cute but noisy cat.